REA

ALLEN COUNTY PUBLIC LIBRARY
Y0-BXV-360

AGAIN, MY LOVE

KAYLA PERRIN

Genesis Press, Inc.

Indigo Love Stories

An imprint of Genesis Press, Inc.
Publishing Company

Genesis Press, Inc.
P.O. Box 101
Columbus, MS 39703

ISBN-13: 978-1-58571-280-9
ISBN-10: 1-58571-280-9
Manufactured in the United States of America

First Edition 1997
Second Edition 2008

Visit us at www.genesis-press.com or call at 1-888-Indigo-1

CHAPTER ONE

She was having the dream again.

That same, torturing dream. The one that caused her heart to race uncontrollably, her breath to come in short, ragged gasps. The dream that had haunted her for what seemed an eternity.

She was locked in a small, dirty room filled with stale air. Approximately twelve-feet by six-feet, it had no windows and felt like a coffin. She was frightened and had been crying, wailing for hours. She had yelled for help until her throat was raw and dry and sore, but nobody came to help her.

Suddenly, the only light in the small room flickered off, and fear gripped her more than ever. Something absolutely frightful.

She opened her mouth to scream, but no sound came out. She tried to move, but to her horror, she realized she was strapped to a bed.

She grew breathless as tears burned her eyes, as panic snared her soul. She had to get out of here. She had to get out before—

"Marcia."

Gasping for air, Marcia Robertson bolted upright. She was sweating, and her eyes bulged with terror. For a moment, she didn't know where she was.

"It's okay." Strong arms wrapped her in a warm embrace. "It was only a bad dream, Marcia."

A bad dream…she was all right. Safe. She was in the arms of her boyfriend, Jackson Reid.

Relieved, she pressed her face against his strong, warm chest. "I was so scared. I—I couldn't move, and they were going to—"

"Shh," he cooed softly, running his fingers along her shoulder-length black hair. "You dozed off and had a bad dream, but it's okay now. Everything's fine."

Everything wasn't fine, and Marcia knew it. She might feel safe for the moment in his arms, but sooner or later the nightmare would return. She'd begun having the dream again right after she had learned of her friend Rachel's pregnancy. Try as she might, her subconscious would not let her close the door on the darkest chapter of her life.

As Jackson continued to hold her, Marcia's breathing calmed. "Thanks, Jackson. I'm better now."

"Good." His relief was audible. "It's almost nine p.m. We have to hurry if we don't want to be late for the party."

The party. She'd forgotten about that. Marcia wasn't really in the mood to go, but there was no way she wanted to stay home alone. Not after the disturbing dream. Maybe music, dancing, and lots of people were exactly what she needed.

"We'd better get ready, then," she said.

He released her from his strong arms, gently cupped her chin, and captured her mouth for a lingering kiss. Her body reacted at once, becoming warm all over. Sliding her hands along Jackson's chest, she started to unbutton his shirt. *This* was exactly what she needed.

Jackson groaned. "Don't do this to me now, baby."

Marcia looked up at him, into his deep brown eyes. He was a beautiful black man. Six-foot-one and lean, yet muscular. A small goatee framed his lips and chin, and his black hair was closely cropped. His skin was dark and smooth and soft to the touch. Her own skin was only slightly lighter, and she loved the way they looked together.

"Why shouldn't I seduce you now?" she asked, her voice husky.

"Because." Jackson captured her hands before she could undo the last two buttons. "You know we can't miss this party."

For a moment longer, she looked at him, hoping. But Jackson was right. This was an important party for anyone in the film business, and they couldn't afford to miss it.

Marcia let out a frustrated sigh, then went to the bathroom to shower. A long, cold shower. Hopefully that would douse the fires until she and Jackson returned home.

The room bubbled with excitement, and Marcia was probably the only person at the party who was bored. She surveyed the room and the various people in it. Everywhere, people were talking, laughing, drinking and mingling with Hollywood stars, yet Marcia felt removed from it all. In spite of the importance of this gathering for film industry moguls, she found herself wishing she had stayed home.

This was the Closing Night Gala for the Toronto International Film Festival, held at a stunningly beautiful top-level complex in an office tower. The women were out in their fanciest gowns, the men in designer tuxedos. Marcia herself was wearing a low-cut black satin dress that shimmered beneath the light.

A waiter in a white shirt and bowtie stopped beside her. "Champagne?"

Accepting a champagne flute off the sterling silver tray, she smiled her thanks. If she must endure the party, she might as well have something to drink.

Marcia brought the delicate crystal flute to her lips and took a long sip as she scanned the room once more. All around her, people were networking, making connections, hoping that a smile and ceaseless chatter would lead to work in an upcoming film. But most of those efforts would prove fruitless. Despite its glamour, the film industry was a tough business. You couldn't trust the men and women behind the friendly smiles unless your contract was already signed on the dotted line, and even then you couldn't trust anyone until the money was in the bank. And, despite the fact that women were ruthlessly used as sex toys, Marcia saw several here tonight flirting madly, no doubt willing to do anything for their elusive "big break."

Thank God she'd never been that pathetic. She believed in working hard, not sleeping her way to the top.

"Marcia!" a man exclaimed, slipping a hand around her waist, then lower, to the small of her back. Any lower and he'd be caressing her buttocks.

Turning sharply, Marcia saw Darryl Dawson, producer, director, and writer. She smiled tightly, then stepped out of his reach. Touchy-feely men were hazards of the film industry, and most of them had no idea they were being offensive.

"Darryl. It's good to see you."

"You've never looked more beautiful."

She knew that was a lie, but replied graciously, "Thank you. You look wonderful, too." Another lie. "How was the screening?"

"Fabulous!" Blue eyes glowing, Darryl ran a hand through his long brown hair. "Not a dry eye in the place. Nor an empty seat. I hope it will be picked up by a distributor."

Marcia had met Darryl Dawson four years earlier through a friend of a friend, when he had just produced his first short film. Now, years later, the ups and downs of the industry hadn't discouraged him, and he had succeeded in producing his first feature film. Marcia had seen the movie the day before and had, in fact, really liked it. She'd also auditioned for the part of the lead actress—a single mother fighting alcohol addiction—but she didn't get the part.

"I wish you luck," she said, smiling. "Even if I still haven't forgiven you for not casting me as Gwen."

"Marcia, I promise you a role in my next feature." He kissed her cheek. "Sorry, dear. Gotta run. There's Stephen Hoffman over there."

She watched him hurry off, a wry grin playing on her lips. She knew there was no way Darryl would cast her in his next film, at least not in a leading role. Although he auditioned people of all ethnic backgrounds, he had cast only Caucasians in the lead roles.

Marcia searched the crowd and finally spotted Jackson, surrounded by several women. Obviously, he was having a good time. *Obviously,* she thought, bitterness washing over her, *he's forgotten that he came to this party with me.*

She released an agitated sigh. She knew she had to share him with others at this party, especially the producers and directors. But observing Jackson now, it bothered her that he wasn't the same person she had met and fallen in love with just over two years ago. Back then, he'd been a down-to-earth actor, praying that one day he'd get something more than bit parts. He had known what it meant to work hard. Now, he was one of the most popular black actors in Toronto, thanks to *The Beat,* an hour-long cop drama in which he had a lead role. Since landing the part of Malcolm Young, his ego had grown by one-hundred-fifty percent.

Marcia was starting toward him when a beautiful, voluptuous blonde approached Jackson and gave him a long hug—a little too long for Marcia's liking. When the woman finally let him go, she still stayed close, touching the front of his shirt in an intimate manner.

Marcia didn't recognize the blonde, but after that hug she could only assume that Jackson knew her. Certainly he wouldn't be that friendly with a random excited fan.

Marcia continued to watch them closely. Jackson clearly didn't seem to be bothered by the curvy woman as he chatted and laughed with her, all the while ignoring everyone else and snatching another glass of champagne from the passing waiter.

Slowly, Marcia wove through the crowd. She smiled at directors, producers, and other actors she knew, but inside she wasn't smiling at all. She was on the verge of seething, truth be told. By now, Jackson should have politely excused himself and left the clinging blonde to her own devices.

She walked right up to Jackson, taking his hand in hers. Smiling at the blonde, she said, "Would you excuse us, please?"

The woman appeared startled, but shrugged and walked away.

"Hi, baby," said Jackson, slurring the words due to too much champagne. "Where've you been all this time?"

Great, Marcia thought. He was drunk. Again, her mind drifted to the Jackson she had known before; that Jackson would never have had too much to drink. That Jackson never got out of control.

"Jackson, I want to go home."

"Oh, c'mon, baby." He wrapped an arm around her shoulder and kissed her temple. "The party's just starting."

"Jackson!" she protested when his mouth moved from her temple to her ear and began nibbling on it.

"Mmm...You taste good."

Marcia squirmed out of his firm grip. "Stop it. You're making a scene."

"Cut!" Jackson laughed at his interpretation of the word "scene." He raised his eyebrows suggestively, desire dancing in his dark eyes. "Let's take this party to a back room."

"No, Jackson. Let's go home. Now."

He snatched another glass of champagne from a waiter, drank it in one gulp and quickly reached for another as the waiter began to walk away.

"Don't you think you've had enough?" asked Marcia, grabbing his arm.

"No, I haven't. I'm doing just fine, baby. Waiter! I'll have another drink here." Jackson pulled his arm from Marcia's grasp and caused her to stumble against someone standing behind her.

A horrified moan escaped from a woman's lips, and, as Marcia whirled around, she could see why. The woman's red wine had spilled all over the front of her white silk dress.

Marcia said, embarrassed, "I'm so sorry."

The woman shot her a disgusted look, muttered something under her breath, and stalked off. Many others were staring at Jackson and Marcia, some merely curious, some just as offended as the wine-doused lady. quite obviously offended.

Marcia had had enough. She glared at Jackson. "Fine. Stay at this party. But you'll have to find your own way home."

She stormed through the crowd of curious onlookers. The spectacle was probably more exciting than some of the scripts they had worked on, and she wasn't about to stay and ruin her chances of ever working in this town again. As she neared the door, she turned to see if Jackson had come to his senses and was following her. To her disappointment, he wasn't.

Marcia walked briskly in the cool September air until she reached the parking lot where her car was parked. It had been a mistake coming here tonight. Now, she just wanted to get home and take a long, hot bath and forget that this night ever happened.

At times like these, Marcia regretted that she had gone against her better judgment and moved in with Jackson. She came from a strict religious household, and while she wasn't perfect, she'd always said she wanted to be married before living with someone. But Jackson had been different. They had connected from the beginning, and she was sure he would be the one she would marry. So, when he suggested living together, Marcia had seen no reason to decline.

She rolled down the car window to get some fresh air as she drove. Maybe she was overreacting. Jackson was basically a good person, and hard working. He had certainly exerted Herculean efforts to make sure that all the casting directors knew who he was and wouldn't hesitate to audition him.

And all his efforts had paid off. Marcia had been thrilled when she learned that Jackson had landed the part of Malcolm Young in *The Beat.* It was the big career break he had been longing for, and it was a regular role at that. That was all any aspiring actor could hope for—a weekly gig that would pay the bills and leave a little extra. *The Beat* paid well, and it was nice for a change for both Jackson and Marcia to live without worrying about how to pay the rent from month to month.

But, with Jackson's sudden success had come problems, problems Marcia feared would ruin their relationship. He was way too busy for her now, which was understandable, considering he often worked twelve-hour days at least four days a week. But she missed the quiet times they used to spend talking, walking in a park, making love. After work, Jackson was too tired to spend any quality time with her and, when he wasn't away working, he was studying his script for the next show.

But she could deal with his schedule. She worked in the business and knew what kind of hours it entailed. What she couldn't deal with was his constant partying and drinking in his free time, as well as his newfound craving for adulation. Jackson no longer seemed happy unless people were stroking his ego, telling him how wonderful an actor he was, and it seemed he particularly craved the attention from especially beautiful, voluptuous women. Where this craving would lead was her worst fear.

Marcia parked in the underground facility of her West End condominium, then took the elevator to the first floor to check the mail.

Bills, she thought sourly, as she flipped through the letters she had retrieved. Only the last item was clearly not a bill. It was a pink-colored card envelope addressed to her. The sender was Gavin Williams.

Gavin! She felt winded suddenly, weak-kneed, almost as though she would faint. Her heart beat a frantic waltz in her chest. Gavin was the last person she had expected to hear from. And she wasn't even sure she wanted to hear from him.

Marcia's stomach tightened. Clutching her mail, she sought the familiar comfort of her and Jackson's modernly furnished apartment. Once there, she marched to the kitchen and the waste can. That was where Gavin's letter belonged. In the trash.

But she couldn't do it. Not without reading it first. Curiosity had always been her besetting sin.

She opened the envelope. Inside was a birthday card. How odd. Gavin knew her birthday had passed two months ago, in July. She flipped open the card and began reading:

Dear Marcia,

You're probably thinking, "A birthday card? It's not my birthday." I know.

I hope you'll accept this card for these past years that I missed your birthday.

I miss you, Marcia, and I'd really like to talk to you again. I think it's time.

Please give me a call at 555-9886. I'd like us to be friends—again.

Sincerely,

Gavin

Marcia re-read the note in a state of total disbelief. A birthday card for all the years he had missed? Was this some kind of joke? He could not possibly expect that she would call him, and certainly not that he could waltz back into her life again after four long years. There was no way she would let that happen. Prior experience with Gavin Williams had taught her a cruel lesson. She preferred to keep the door closed forever on that chapter of her life.

Marcia's hands were shaking from a surge of adrenaline. Ripping the card and envelope into shreds, she dropped them into the waste can. But she could not rid herself of memories as easily as she could of the card. For three extraordinary years, Marcia had loved Gavin; they'd even planned their wedding. But his love had not been unconditional. When she was forced to face the truth and their relationship ended, she'd been devastated. She had suffered a pain so deep she hadn't known if she would survive. There was no way they could ever be friends. The scars were too deep.

Marcia curled up on the black leather sofa in her living room and hugged her knees to her chest. She felt emotionally numb, overwhelmed by the shock of hearing from Gavin again. Why, after four years, did it matter to him if they ever spoke again? The more she thought about him and his card, the angrier she felt. The anger was not directed at Gavin alone, but at herself as well for wasting so much time and emotional energy on an episode in her life that was in the past and should be forgotten. Should be…but could not.

Neither the bad, nor the good and beautiful. It all lingered.

"You must think I'm a complete fool, Gavin," Marcia said aloud.

Her past with him was dead and buried, and there was no way she was going to dig up all the painful memories. Not after the private hell she had endured, and all it had taken her to get to this point in her life.

No way in hell.

CHAPTER TWO

Seven years ago…

"What's your name?" he asked, his dazzling smile causing her heart to flutter.

"Marcia," she replied shyly, then giggled. She didn't know why she was laughing and hoped that he didn't think she was too immature. The truth was, when she was shy, she always giggled.

"I'm Gavin." He extended his hand, and she shook it.

Marcia leaned against the porch railing to steady herself. Man, he was fine! And tall. He towered over her, and she was five-foot-eight.

"How tall are you?" she asked, immediately thinking her question was dumb.

He smiled at her again, and she thought she would die. "I'm six-four."

"Holy!" Marcia couldn't contain the outburst. She knew she was acting like a giddy teenager, even though she was twenty years old. If she wanted to impress him, she would have to control herself.

"I get that reaction a lot. Does that mean you like it?"

Marcia was momentarily caught off guard, but then she realized what he was asking her. "Like it? Oh—of course. I love tall men. Well, not all of them...you know what I mean."

Gavin chuckled softly, and Marcia's face grew warm. He did think she was immature! Darn. She'd been trying so hard to be cool and collected.

"I think you're cute."

Her small frown was instantly replaced by a beaming ear-to-ear smile. Before she blurted out something silly, she thought better of it and merely said, "Thanks."

Joining her at the railing, he crossed his ankles. "I don't want to seem forward, but could I get your number? I'd really like to talk to you again."

Yes! her mind yelled. Then she said coolly, "Sure."

She extracted a piece of paper from her purse and wrote down her number. Marcia couldn't help but wonder what she had done to be so lucky. He was the most gorgeous man she had ever seen, and he had a smile that could melt ice cream. She knew at that very moment that she was in love.

He tore off a piece of the paper she had given him, wrote his number on it, then passed it back to her. A soft giggle threatened to escape, but she managed to suppress it. She was so happy, she could have jumped for joy right there on the spot.

"Do you need a ride home?" he asked, his sexy brown eyes holding hers captive.

"No," Marcia responded. "I came with—" She looked toward the sidewalk, but to her amazement, her sister and her best friend were gone. So was the car.

Oh, they were clever, setting her up like this! They were the ones who had pointed out that the best-looking man at the barbecue was staring at her. She'd been too shy to approach him, and now this!

"Uh—it seems my sister has left me, so…sure. I do need a ride home after all."

Marcia knew without question that Gavin was a gentleman and would never try to take advantage of her. When he drove her home, he was sweet and polite, and when he stopped in front of her parents' house, he didn't even try to kiss her.

"I'll call you later tonight," he said in that deep sexy voice of his, and once again Marcia was thankful that she didn't melt on the spot.

He called her that night, just as he said, and then the next night, then the next. He never stopped calling her, and pretty soon, they were officially a couple. Three years her senior, he lived in a campus dorm at the university he attended. There were plenty of times Marcia could have, and, in fact, wanted to stay over, but Gavin never asked. He always called her his "queen" and said that she deserved to be respected, and that they would both know when the time was right.

Marcia's leg fell off the sofa and hit the floor, jolting her awake. Groaning, she sat up and buried her face in her hands. She'd been dreaming. About Gavin. How could she? She was happy with Jackson.

Jackson…had he come home? She ran to the bedroom. He wasn't there, and the bedside clock showed eight a.m. Marcia's heart sank. In the year that they had lived together he had not once failed to come home. She had become accustomed to his warm body at night and the security that it brought.

Maybe Jackson's absence was why she had dreamed of Gavin.

But that was a thought she could not tolerate. Restless, Marcia sashayed to the window and opened the blinds. The sun was shining brilliantly, and it warmed her face through the glass. She surveyed the ground below, watching the people coming and going from the building, wondering when Jackson would get home.

She felt a pang of guilt. She shouldn't have left him at the party in the condition he was in, but he'd just made her so mad. He'd been obnoxious and impossible to talk to, not to mention made a spectacle of her to the onlookers. Still, she had expected him to come home last night.

Maybe he had stayed with Jeff, his agent and personal manager. Ever since Jackson had landed his big role, Jeff had been one of his best friends. It was still early, and no doubt Jackson was hung over. She would just have to wait for him to come home. Sober and rested, he should be able to understand that his drunken behavior was causing problems.

She spent some time rehearsing rational arguments to bring up with Jackson, but the dream-images of Gavin kept intruding. He had been so romantic, and she had loved him so much. Despite the four years that had passed and the fact that they hadn't been in touch since the breakup, their relationship was one Marcia could hardly forget.

But then, wasn't there always something special, something unforgettable about a first love? She had been so young when she'd fallen in love with Gavin, a mere twenty compared to his twenty-three years. She had been naive in many ways. She had been giddy and excited, the way only a young girl could be about her first true love. She was twenty-seven now, and had matured. Indeed, Gavin had taught her cruel lessons as well as beautiful ones. No one but Gavin had ever given her so much pleasure. Or so much pain.

Marcia swallowed the lump that had unexpectedly formed in her throat. She had to stop this impromptu trip down memory lane. It would do no good to stir up reminders of past anguish.

Marcia showered and dressed. Still no Jackson. And she had been looking forward to spending this Sunday together, doing something—anything—together.

Unsettled, Marcia wandered through the apartment. She suddenly remembered the answering machine. Maybe Jackson had called while she was in the shower. Moving across the living room to the answering machine, she saw that the message light was indeed flashing. Her finger pounced on the play button.

There were two messages—one from her best friend, Lonita Henry, and one from her sister, Andrea. Nothing from Jackson. She didn't know whether to be concerned or angry.

She rewound the messages. Lonita had merely said to call her, while her sister had gone on about some crisis with a current boyfriend for which she needed Marcia's immediate advice.

Marcia groaned softly, contemplating which of the two to call first. Talking to her sister meant a long conversation, and she was in no mood to solve her sister's love life. Not when her own love life was foremost on her mind.

She dialed Lonita's number. Lonita answered after two rings.

"Lonita, it's Marcia."

"Oh, hi. What's up, girl?"

"I'm returning your call. So, what's up with you?"

Lonita laughed. "You know me. I'm dying to hear the scoop about the big party last night."

Marcia was tempted to confide in her friend, but perhaps she ought to wait until she had spoken with Jackson. "It was okay."

"Okay? That's all?"

"It was nothing to write home about."

"Girlfriend, what's going on with you? You were at a party with Hollywood stars and it was 'nothing to write home about'? I know if I had been there with one of the nation's hottest stars, not to mention one of the best-looking ones, I would still be on cloud nine."

It's different when that star is your boyfriend, Marcia thought. Instead, she said, "This business isn't all it's cracked up to be sometimes, that's all."

"What's the matter, Marcia? And don't tell me 'nothing.'"

Marcia couldn't easily fool Lonita, who had been her best friend since fourth grade. Still, she tried. "I'm just tired. It was a long night."

"Nice try, but I know something else is wrong." Lonita paused before asking, "Is it Jackson?"

The question momentarily rendered Marcia speechless, even though she knew how perceptive Lonita was.

"That's it, isn't it? You and Jackson had a fight?"

"I guess you could say that," Marcia admitted. "But it's really nothing major." She explained what had happened the previous night, and how Jackson had not come home yet.

"Girl, I thought it was worse than that."

"I told you it was nothing."

"Then something else is wrong. Start talking, Marcia And don't even try lying, because I know you too well."

Marcia couldn't help but smile, which was a first for the day. Lonita did know her well. It was wonderful to have a friend who was so in tune with your personality that she knew when something was out of whack. It could also pose a problem at times when you didn't want to discuss what was bothering you.

"If you must know," Marcia began slowly, "there is something else. I got a card yesterday, and you'll never guess from whom."

"Gavin."

Marcia frowned at the phone receiver in her hand. Perceptive Lonita might be, but she was not clairvoyant.

"You certainly don't seem to be surprised," said Marcia, her voice tight. "I think it's you who has to start talking."

"I didn't think he'd send you a card."

"You gave Gavin my address!"

"Now, don't get upset. He would have gotten it one way or another."

"So, why did you have to give it to him then? If I had wanted him to know where I am—"

"Just hear me out," Lonita said, cutting Marcia off.

"And when were you going to tell me about this?"

"Hold up, Marcia!" Lonita's tone was forceful. "First of all, I didn't just give him your address. I saw him at the mall, and we started talking. Then he asked about you, how you were doing, if you were still acting. He told me that he had something of yours that he wanted to send to you. I figured it was no big deal, since I told him that you were involved in a serious relationship. If I had known he was lying to me, I wouldn't have told him anything."

Lonita's explanation satisfied Marcia. "Can you believe the man expects me to call him? After four years?"

"He also said that he wasn't in Toronto for the past three years. He was in—you'll never believe this—Japan. Teaching English."

"Really?"

"Mmmhmm."

Marcia digested the information. During their last year together, Gavin had graduated from Teacher's College, but he hadn't been able to get a job. He could only get on a supply list, and that hadn't satisfied him. Only a classroom of his own would do that.

Pensively, she said, "He always wanted to be a teacher."

"That explains why you haven't heard from him for so long, right?"

But it wasn't enough. Marcia had no right to feel like this, but she felt betrayed. Gavin had left the country and never even thought about letting her know what he was doing. True, their relationship had ended. True, he didn't know her address in Vancouver…

"Marcia, did you hear me?"

"I'm sorry. What did you say?"

"I said, that explains why you haven't heard from him for so long."

"I—I guess so."

There was silence on the other end of the line before Lonita said, "There's no harm in getting to know him again. You two were so close. It's really a shame how things ended."

"No," Marcia said sharply. "I want nothing to do with him."

"I'm sorry. I didn't know it would upset you this much. If I had—"

"I'm not upset." Marcia's brusque tone said otherwise. She forced a smile. "Let's just forget about it, okay?"

"All right." Lonita's voice was perky once again. "Listen, Marcia. I've gotta run. Let's hook up tonight, if you're free."

"I'll see."

Marcia hung up the phone, then stood for several moments, dazed and confused about what she had learned. Gavin had gone to Japan to teach. He'd gone on with his life.

Without her.

But so had she. Without him.

"Big deal if you left town and never told me," she said aloud. "There are several things I haven't told you, Gavin."

Like the secret she had kept from him.

The secret she hadn't told anybody.

The secret that was so painful she still found it hard to face her reflection in the mirror each morning when she rose to greet the day.

CHAPTER THREE

By six o'clock in the evening, Jackson still wasn't home. Marcia was fuming. Any feeling of guilt about leaving him at the party in his drunken condition had long since turned to anger.

He should have called her. Even if he was as angry with her as she was with him, he owed her the courtesy of a phone call.

I should call Gavin, she thought, just out of spite.

Startled by the unexpected and totally undesirable turn her thoughts had taken, Marcia pressed her hands to her heated face. His card lay shredded at the bottom of the kitchen waste can, but the number he had written on the card was indelibly etched in her mind. It didn't matter. She certainly would not call him. She had nothing to say to him.

She picked up the phone and called her sister, Andrea.

"Where have you been?" Andrea blurted out. "I thought you had died!"

Marcia smiled. Her younger sister had always had a flair for the dramatic. She should have been the actress. Instead, Andrea held down a regular nine-to-five job as a secretary at an advertising firm.

"Well, I'm not dead," Marcia announced needlessly. "What's up with you, or should I say, with Curtis?"

"He hasn't called me in three days!"

Marcia sat quietly, waiting for her sister to expand. When her sister said nothing, Marcia asked, "Is that all?"

"Is that all?" Andrea wailed. "What do you mean? Isn't that enough reason for me to be worried?"

"How many other times has he done this?" Marcia answered her own question. "Five hundred? A thousand? Really, Andrea! Aren't you used to this by now?"

"Oh, so because he's done it before, I shouldn't be upset about it."

"No," Marcia said slowly, determined to make her sister see the point. "Since he's done it before, you should be used to it. You've either got to kick him to the curb, or you've got to put up with it. I know that if he were my man, he'd be gone."

"Well, this is the last time he's playing me for a fool. I'm through with him! I don't need that man in my life!"

Marcia almost chuckled aloud. For as long as her sister had been dating Curtis, she was threatening to dump him. Curtis was her first real love, and Marcia understood all too well what kind of hold that could have on a person. But Curtis didn't seem to understand the first thing about respecting a woman. He would disappear for days on end without even calling, leaving Andrea sick with worry. Then, suddenly he would show up at her door, apologize for being too "busy" to call, and Andrea would happily take him back. It was a sickening cycle.

Marcia had no doubt where Curtis was when he disappeared for several days. He was either married, or he was seeing someone else. Marcia had tried to tell her sister that, but Andrea just didn't want to believe it.

"Well, girl," Marcia said to her sister, "I hope you mean it this time. That man doesn't deserve you."

"I do mean it. You wait and see. If he thinks he can treat me like this and get away with it time and time again..."

Marcia listened to her sister babble on about how she was going to dump Curtis, how he was a no-good louse, and how she could find several other guys worthy of her love. It was the same old song Marcia had heard time and time again, but she bit her tongue and let Andrea talk until she ran out of steam. Despite all her sister's ranting, Marcia knew she wasn't ready to dump Curtis.

A wry smile curved Marcia's mouth. The sex must be mighty good.

They finally ended the conversation, with Marcia promising to meet Andrea and Lonita later at The Palace, a nightclub they enjoyed going to on occasion. The place was usually packed Thursday through Sunday.

Normally, Marcia didn't go out much—and she wasn't really in the mood to go out again after last night's disastrous party—but since Jackson didn't feel the need to call or come home, she wasn't about to stay at home like a pitiable fool and wait for him.

At nine o'clock, Marcia was dressed in a black miniskirt and a red satin top. She looked good. Secretly, she hoped that Jackson would walk through the door as she was leaving so he could see what he was missing. But he didn't show up. She was angrier than ever now and even more determined to have a good time.

By nine-thirty, Marcia had picked up Lonita, then her sister, whose apartment wasn't too far from the club. All three women looked fine. Lonita wore a body-hugging black dress that flattered her voluptuous figure. Andrea, who was slim but also well proportioned, wore black tights with a white tank top. No doubt they would get a lot of attention from the men in the club—they always did.

"I hope I see Curtis here," Andrea announced as they stood in line waiting to get into the club. "If I see him, I'll give him a piece of my mind."

Lonita shot Marcia a knowing look.

When they entered the club, a popular reggae tune was playing, and the crowd was ecstatic. People blew whistles, waved their hands in the air, and danced in all the latest reggae styles. In dark corners, and even under bright lights, couples were grinding their bodies together, moving rhythmically with the music.

Even though she was mad at him, Marcia wished Jackson were here with her tonight.

"Let's go to the bar," Lonita suggested over the loud music.

In a crowd like this, they had to walk single file, which made three unaccompanied young women easy prey to men on the prowl. Lonita, who was single, liked the attention, but Marcia didn't need the type of attention the men at a club like this gave her. Sure, she was human and she was flattered by admiration just like any other woman, but she certainly didn't need to flirt to make herself feel good.

Marcia was sipping on a piña colada when Andrea asked her, "Isn't that Jackson?"

Marcia immediately pulled the straw from her mouth and asked, "Jackson? Where?" Her heart started to beat a little faster. If Jackson was here, maybe they could resolve their differences and make up for last night.

"I see him," said Lonita.

Marcia craned her neck to see where her sister and her friend were pointing.

And then she saw him.

Jackson, dressed in a sharp red blazer and black pants, was hard to miss at his height. He was on the dance floor. With another woman. Dancing wholeheartedly to a funky tune.

A queasy sensation overtook Marcia. She took several deep breaths, but that did nothing to make her feel better. How could Jackson do this to her? He hadn't seen fit to come home all day, or to call her and let her know he was still alive. Yet here he was, carefree on a dance floor, dancing with another woman.

Marcia walked toward the dance floor. Her stomach was still in knots, but she couldn't let this one slide. She had to confront him.

As she got closer, she recognized the woman dancing with Jackson. It was Camille, a black woman with whom Marcia was slightly acquainted. If memory served her right, Camille was a receptionist at one of the major casting houses. Her hair was cut in a short bob, and she looked very attractive in a green sheath dress. Marcia's heart began to race. She'd always suspected that Camille liked Jackson, but to her knowledge, Camille respected their relationship, or so she thought.

"Jackson," Marcia said when she finally reached him, her tone flat.

The wide smile he was directing at Camille disappeared, and his expression changed to surprise as he realized Marcia was standing next to him.

"I need to talk to you, Jackson." She looked toward Camille and with difficulty forced a smile. "Will you excuse us?"

Camille looked at Jackson, who said, "Gimme a minute, please." With a shrug, he faced Marcia. "Okay. Let's talk."

"Not here."

Marcia took his hand and led him through the crowd to a less populated area near the washrooms. Crossing her arms, she leaned her back against a wall. She said nothing, only gave him a level stare.

Jackson broke the silence. "I didn't think you wanted to have anything to do with me."

"And why is that?" Her voice held a hint of challenge.

"After the way you left me last night—"

"Oh, come on, Jackson. You refused to leave with me, even after embarrassing us both. You gave me no choice."

"See? I knew you were still mad."

Marcia willed herself to remain composed. "I was mad. I'm not anymore. But I'm not happy that you didn't even call me for the entire day, and now you're out here with Camille."

"She's just a friend."

"That's not the point. The point is that I was worried."

"You were so worried that you decided to dance the night away," he replied, his tone dripping with sarcasm.

Marcia shot him a look of distaste. "I'm here with Andrea and Lonita. What did you expect? That I'd sit at home sulking? I certainly have a right to go out, too, now don't I?"

"Is this why you dragged me over here? To have an argument and cause a scene?"

Marcia drew in a deep breath and counted to five. "No. I'm sorry. Jackson, I don't want us to fight. Can't we just forget yesterday and move on?"

When he didn't respond, she took a step toward him. Placing a hand lightly on his shoulder, she looked into his eyes. "Jackson?"

"Yes, of course," he said quickly.

She kept looking at him because his tone didn't match his words, and she found it hard to take comfort in what he said. He seemed mad at her, which was strange since she was the one with the reason to be angry. But she did not want to fight any longer.

Softly, Marcia stroked Jackson's goatee. "Why don't we just go home—"

"I came here with Camille. I can't just leave her."

Marcia snatched back her hand as if she had been bitten by a snake. "I see."

"I gave her a ride here. She'll be stranded if I leave her."

Marcia swallowed a sharp retort. "All right. I'll see you at home."

"Yeah, I'll see you." Evading her steady gaze, he surveyed the area nearby to see if Camille was still patiently waiting. She was. Planting a quick kiss on Marcia's cheek, he strode off to join the other woman.

Marcia watched him go, a numb feeling spreading through her body. Something wasn't right.

She needed air. She needed to get out. She needed to get away from Jackson. Head bent, looking neither right nor left, she sped toward the main entrance of the club. In her haste, she bumped right into somebody.

"I'm sorry," she said, looking up.

Her eyes widened and her mouth fell open in shock.

"Marcia." His voice was deep and sexy as her name spilled from his lips. "We finally meet again."

CHAPTER FOUR

Marcia closed her eyes, positive that when she reopened them, she would find her mind had been playing tricks on her.

But it hadn't. It was Gavin.

He smiled at her. "Aren't you going to say hi?"

"G-Gavin." Her breathing was none too steady. "What are you doing here?"

He shrugged. "Just a night out with the boys. I thought I would enjoy myself before I get really bogged down with the school year."

"School?" Marcia asked, her mind frazzled because of this unexpected meeting.

"Yeah, I'm teaching. Did you get my card?"

Marcia inhaled a deep breath and was relieved that her lungs allowed it. "I—yes. Gavin, I was on my way out. I need some air."

"Are you sick?" Concerned, he extended his arm. "Let me help you."

She accepted. She didn't want Jackson to see her talking with another man. But then again, maybe she did.

Gavin led her through the front doors and out into the parking lot. He stopped when they reached a late model bright red Ford Mustang.

Marcia took her hand off Gavin's arm and hugged her body.

"Is this your car?"

"Yeah. This is my baby. Two months old."

Marcia stole a glance at him. He looked the same as she had remembered him, clean-shaven, oval-shaped face, dark brown eyes, golden brown skin. His hair was shorter than he used to wear it, but nicely styled—as always. He still had those gorgeous dimples when he smiled. And his body—He had the muscular build of an athlete, evident even beneath a black silk shirt and tan pants. The shirt's top three buttons were undone, and Marcia could see the smooth, golden skin of his chest. He was still as beautiful as the day she'd met him so long ago.

"Marcia, would you like to sit down?"

At the sound of his voice, she lifted her eyes to his face. "No. No, thank you. I have to go. I've got people waiting for me inside."

"They'll be there when you return." Before she could move, he reached out and took a few strands of her hair between his fingers and played with them. In doing so, his fingers brushed against her face. The light touch alerted every nerve in Marcia's body, reminding her of the way it used to be.

"I have to go," she repeated, her voice unsteady. "They'll be wondering where I am."

"I only want a few minutes of your time."

"Why?"

Gavin crossed his arms, those beautifully sculpted arms, rippling with muscles acquired through diligent weight training. Everything about him was still so sexy, still so tempting.

"I'd like to know if you were planning to call me."

Her mind whirled. Why did she have to run into him again? Why was she light-headed at the mere touch of his fingers? Seeing him without warning had caught her off guard. That was the problem. She just needed to pull herself together, collect her wits.

"Marcia, are you going to answer the question, or am I to assume that your silence means—"

"Don't assume anything," she said curtly. "That was always your problem. You assumed way too much."

"Okay," Gavin conceded. "Then why don't you answer my question."

"If you want to know the truth, I didn't plan to call you. I didn't plan to talk to you ever again. Well, that's impossible now, since we're already talking. Not that I know what to say. Frankly, Gavin, I'm still getting over the shock that you decided to contact me after all this time."

Gavin nodded somberly. "It has been a long time, Marcia. I can certainly understand how this is unexpected. But I needed to talk to you again, to see you. Lately, I haven't been able to get you off my mind. I guess I thought that we could…try and get close again."

"Is that so?" she asked sharply, regretting more and more that she had run into him. "And what's different now from four years ago? Why on earth would you even consider getting acquainted with me again, much less get close to me? I am still the same person, Gavin. Still an actress."

"Can't we just forget the past?"

Marcia stared at him. "You cannot be serious! How can you expect me to forget the past? I was the one who got the raw end of the deal! You have no idea what I went through."

"I didn't mean that the way it sounded. I know I made mistakes, and the biggest mistake I made was letting you go."

"You didn't let me go," Marcia snapped. "You left me no choice but to go."

"I know, and I'm sorry."

"You're sorry?" She wanted to laugh in his face. Wanted to cry. In the end, she merely backed away from him. "That's great, Gavin. That's just great."

"Don't go, Marcia."

Gavin closed the distance between them in one quick stride, and she was all too aware of the powerful magnetism he had always exuded to her. Even his alluring scent was the same as she remembered it.

Turning abruptly, she started for the club. She needed to get away from her past. Needed to see Jackson, her anchor to the present. But he was with Camille—or had left to take her home.

Marcia felt deserted, alone, then she remembered Lonita and Andrea. She walked faster, and when Gavin placed a hand on her shoulder to detain her, she shrugged him off.

He fell into step beside her. "Whether or not you believe me, I am truly sorry for hurting you. It wasn't a picnic for me either when you decided to leave—"

"You mean, when you forced me to leave."

"Okay. I guess you're right."

"You guess I'm right?" Marcia had had enough. She couldn't bear to be with him any longer. At the club entrance, she faced him briefly. "Gavin, I'm glad you're fine. I'm glad you're teaching. I'm glad you realized your dream. Goodbye and good luck."

"You've got every right to be mad at me, Marcia. All I'm asking you is to give me a chance to make it up to you."

"I'm sorry, Gavin. I'm in love with someone else."

Gavin watched her go, his mind still reeling from the shock her words had caused.

Frustrated, he ran a hand over his hair. What had he expected her to say? That everything was forgiven and that she loved him and wanted him back? What a fool he had been, too hopeful, and more than a little unrealistic.

Yet now that he had seen her again, he knew without a doubt that he had never stopped loving her. Her long slender legs, her soft full lips, her thickly lashed eyes, her soft, supple skin…she was just as he had remembered her. Except now there was a sadness in her eyes. A sadness he knew he had caused her.

He didn't feel like staying at the club. Two of his friends were inside, but they had driven their own cars. He jumped into his Mustang, revved the engine and zipped out of the parking lot at a speed that was unnecessarily fast. But no speed was fast enough to outrun the memories tumbling in his mind.

CHAPTER FIVE

Six-and-a-half years ago…

She lay in his arms under a weeping willow tree, basking in the afterglow of their lovemaking. This was their first time together, and it was magical. Gavin proved to be sensitive, passionate, and romantic. It was his idea to take a picnic basket and some wine to a secluded area of High Park for some romance.

There, they dined on strawberries and chocolate-covered almonds, and shared a glass of wine. The entire time, Marcia knew that their lovemaking would be the grand finale, and the mystery of what was to come, of how he would love her, thrilled her.

Before Gavin, Marcia had had one sexual experience—a loveless encounter that had fallen short of her expectations. After that, she couldn't understand what the big deal was about sex.

But with Gavin, it was different. His kisses alone set her skin on fire. His eyes made her heart race. At night, he invaded her dreams.

But even her dreams fell short of the reality. Gavin thrilled her in every way, made her feel the most wonderful, exciting sensations. He took her to a place so magical, so filled with love, that she could only marvel. Beneath the weeping willow, they were one with nature, one with each other. Two bodies, one soul, joined in a song of love.

Marcia had found her soul mate in Gavin.

Marcia stirred, arching her back—and woke up. She was alone in the bed she and Jackson usually shared. Her skin felt hot, her breasts taut. Her whole body ached for the release that only lovemaking could bring.

The sound of the key turning in the door startled her, and Marcia scrambled under the covers. She had been so caught up in dreams and memories that she lost track of time. It was shortly after three a.m., and she'd been home for over an hour. Waiting for Jackson.

She hadn't expected to take a trip down memory lane.

She heard the apartment door close. Jackson peeked into the bedroom, where the lamp on her night table cast a soft, romantic glow. Marcia had set up this seduction scene and dressed in a sexy white negligee to signal that all was forgiven. That she loved Jackson dearly.

But now, as he approached her, she wondered about her feelings. About why, if she truly loved Jackson, she couldn't get Gavin out of her mind.

Jackson eased himself onto the bed beside her, smiling as he pulled back the covers. He ran his fingers along her leg, bent it when he reached her knee, then pressed his mouth to her flesh, moistening it with his tongue.

But instead of exciting her, as it normally would have, his touch evoked no response. Suddenly, Marcia knew that she couldn't go through with her plan to seduce Jackson. Not tonight.

Something wasn't right, and she was no longer in the mood. Almost immediately, anger washed over her—anger with herself and her sudden inability to return Jackson's affection. He was ready to make amends, and she should have been ready, too. But she wasn't.

Jackson trailed a moist path along her leg, edging ever nearer to her center of pleasure.

She reached out and placed her hand on his head. "Jackson...don't."

He raised his head and flashed her a perplexed look.

"I'm sorry," Marcia said, feeling horrible for doing this to him. "It's late now, and I'm just so tired. Could you just...hold me?"

Jackson said nothing, merely stared at her for several moments. Marcia knew that she had sent him a mixed message. But she couldn't make love to him unless her heart was truly in it.

"Please," she said, her voice soft.

He let out a faint sigh, then stretched out beside her and took her in his arms. She cuddled against him and wished this night could have been different.

Wished she could get Gavin out of her mind.

Bright morning sun shining through the blinds and spilling onto the bed woke Marcia. The digital clock on the bedside table read sixteen minutes past ten.

She rose, stretched, then went to the closet. Slipping into a robe, she asked Jackson, "When is your call time?"

Slowly, he rolled over onto his back. "Noon."

"Would you like some breakfast?" Marcia hoped he wasn't upset about last night. She felt truly horrible that she hadn't been able to make love with him. "An omelet?"

"Sounds great." Yawning, Jackson stretched.

He didn't look upset, Marcia noted. But he was quite possibly possibly bored. Or indifferent? Perhaps that was worse than upset.

Mulling over the events of the past days, Marcia prepared an omelet with freshly diced tomatoes, chopped mushrooms and cheddar cheese. That was Jackson's favorite. For herself, she made scrambled eggs and toast.

They sat together at the dining table in the solarium, the sun warm on their faces. Jackson ate heartily, which pleased Marcia.

"I'm sorry about last night," she blurted out.

He shrugged, his attention on his food. "Don't worry about it. I certainly know what it's like to be tired."

Marcia eyed him, wondering what was going on in his mind. He hadn't even looked at her when he replied. How were they going to work this out?

The telephone rang. Marcia sighed, deploring the phone's timing. She scurried to answer before the third ring.

"Hi, Michael," she said when she heard her agent's voice on the other end of the receiver. "Oh. Okay, great." She grabbed a pen and started scribbling. "Ten forty-five...and what's the part?" Marcia scribbled down more information. "Sounds good...and you'll fax the sides? Thanks...thanks a lot. Bye."

Dropping the receiver, she rushed to Jackson. "Guess what, hon?"

"You've got an audition?"

"Finally." She slipped her arms around him in a quick, spontaneous hug. "It's for a feature film coming up from the States. And it sounds like an interesting part. But, hey, anything's better than what I've been getting recently."

Which was exactly nothing. She had suffered a dry spell, with the last audition being a month ago. The role in a shampoo commercial was wonderful because it paid residuals, but still, she hated sitting around the apartment, unable to do what she loved most in the world.

The fax line rang; Marcia's agent was faxing her the copy of the script she needed for the audition.

"Well, what's the part?" Jackson asked.

"A lawyer in a private law firm. If I get it, my agent says it will be five days' work." Marcia smiled widely, knowing how much money a five-day job could bring in. She wanted to work—needed to work. Not just for the money, but also to keep her creative juices flowing. "I've just got to get this part!"

"You'll get it." Jackson squeezed her hand.

Her eyes misted at this sudden show of affection. She and Jackson would work things out.

She said, "The audition's the day after tomorrow, which gives me only two days to learn the lines. Do you think you'll have time to go over the script with me?"

"Hopefully." Jackson took a swig of apple juice. "Tomorrow's going to be a long day, though. We're filming a car chase scene. I don't know when I'll get home."

Marcia would be lucky if Jackson had half an hour to help her when he got home. He worked long hours and was always exhausted afterward. She could only hope.

She collected their plates, rinsed them in the kitchen, then dashed into the spare bedroom where the fax was.

There were four pages of dialogue, which she carried into the living room. She sat on the sofa and silently began reading the lines.

"It's pretty dramatic," she said, intrigued as she scanned the scene. "The lawyer is being questioned by the FBI about her law firm's activities."

Jackson joined her on the sofa, his head close to hers as he read along.

"Great!" Marcia's eyes widened with interest. "She freaks out by the end of it. I can do that. I love auditions with a high drama level. Those are my best!"

"Hon, this is you." Jackson kissed her cheek. "You'll get this one." He hopped off the sofa and headed for the bedroom.

Marcia wished they could have spent more time together, but it was late and Jackson had to get ready. A driver would pick him up in less than an hour.

Forty-five minutes later, they had both showered and dressed. Marcia kissed Jackson deeply before he ran down to the waiting car. But the kiss wasn't what she had hoped it would be; it didn't heat her blood as it used to.

The phone rang. She was slow in answering it, her mind troubled by the less than satisfactory kiss she had exchanged with Jackson. Was it her fault that there hadn't been a spark? Or was it his?

The phone continued to ring, annoying her with its persistence. When she finally picked up the receiver, her voice reflected her ruffled feelings. "Hello!"

"Don't tell me I've caught you at a bad time."

Marcia froze. She knew that voice all too well.

Gavin!

CHAPTER SIX

Marcia could not believe her ears. Was Gavin actually on the other end of her line?

"I realize you're busy, Marcia, but I won't be long." Gavin's voice reverberated through the phone line.

Yes, this was real. Marcia swallowed. "What do you want?"

"I need to see you."

"I'm sorry, Gavin. That's impossible."

"Marcia." His voice was deep and compelling. "Let me see you today. Please."

The sound of his voice had her head spinning. She'd had a hard time saying no to him in the past, and she felt her resolve slipping. "Why?"

"Because we need to talk, Marcia. And one way or another, we will. If you don't agree to meet me, I'm warning you now that I'll show up at your apartment. So make your decision. Do you want to meet me at your place, or somewhere else?"

"What kind of choice is that?"

"The only kind that will get me what I want."

She could hear a smile in his voice, but that kind of choice reminded her all too painfully of the ultimatum he had given her that dreadful day four years ago.

"Come on, Marcia. Say yes."

"You really haven't changed at all, Gavin. You've always been like this. You've always felt that you were to be listened to, that your way was the only way. Well, forget it! I'm not going to see you today—not ever."

She hung up and stood motionless for several seconds. Where had that strength come from? One minute her resolve started to slip, the next she was slamming the phone in his ear.

It was the memory of their breakup that had given her the sudden surge of strength. It always was too painful for her to bear. To this day, she wondered if she had made the right choice when she left Gavin. His ultimatum had been so sudden, so unexpected, but she hadn't wanted to give in to him. At the time, she'd thought that she could get over him, but she'd been wrong. Lord, how she had suffered. She couldn't help wondering how her life would be different now if she had declined the part in Vancouver and had stayed here in Toronto with Gavin.

And it would have been different. She would have been completely miserable, wondering what might have been, what she could have achieved. Even though the choice she made had brought with it agony, her decision had been necessary for her own progress.

Just as it was necessary now to stay away from Gavin.

Gavin sat at the broad oak desk in his classroom long after the students had left. He wanted to see Marcia. Lord knew, he needed to see her.

He leaned back in his plush swivel chair, closed his eyes, and stretched. Even the students in his fifth-grade class had noticed that something was bothering him, and many had asked him what was wrong.

What was wrong was that he couldn't get Marcia out of his system. Now that he had secured a full-time job as a teacher, his mind had started drifting to his past life and to his former dreams.

Marcia had been there in all those dreams.

For three years, he had loved her, and he had been certain that he would love her for eternity. He wanted to marry her once he'd gotten himself established in a school and started making some real money. But he hadn't found a full-time job and had become more than a little frustrated.

When he thought back on the breakup, he accepted the fact that he had failed to be completely open with Marcia, and that it was that failure that led to their parting. He hadn't minded the fact that she loved acting, but in the back of his mind, that kind of a career scared him. His own father had been a musician, and his father's artistic career had been the reason for his parents' divorce. His father hadn't wanted to be tied down, and his mother hadn't wanted to live a life on the road. Subconsciously, Gavin had feared that he and Marcia would suffer the same fate if she remained an actress.

That was precisely why he had forced her to make a decision just when she'd gotten her big break. She had been so excited when she told him the news, but he had literally frozen, gripped by fear. He had felt the hairs rise at the back of his neck, and he knew he was going to lose her the way he had lost his father.

Damn, if only he could turn back the clock. She had loved him so much and she'd been devastated when he backed her into a corner. He had expected her to say "no" to a wonderful opportunity—to choose him over her career. When she didn't do as he had expected, he had refused to call her, thinking that for sure she would be intimidated into declining the role. He'd been positive she would call him and tell him that she had changed her mind.

He had waited a year for that call. It was painfully obvious by then that she had made her decision, that she hadn't chosen him. As time passed, he learned she was already in Vancouver filming a new television series. He'd felt betrayed by her decision, and had refused to watch any of the episodes of her show. He'd sulked around the house for a year, missing her desperately, until he finally realized that he needed to leave town. He couldn't stay any longer where the memories were so fresh, the pain so raw.

So, on a whim, and at his mother's urging, he had gone to Japan to teach English. The pay rate was great, and after initially planning to stay for a year, one year had turned into two; two had turned into three. Then his mother took ill with cancer, and he tendered his resignation and returned to Canada to be by her side.

Thank God his mother was all right now; the cancerous lump had been successfully removed from her breast. He wouldn't leave her again; he couldn't. She was still weak from the radiation and chemotherapy treatments, and she needed him.

Since his return, he had been busy taking care of his mother and busy with applications to various school boards. He expected to be placed on a supply list again, but surprisingly, an opening emerged in the Etobicoke Board of Education, and he was asked to fill it. Again, he stayed busy…first with preparations, then getting to know his students. And now…

Now, since realizing his dream of becoming a teacher, all his thoughts centered on Marcia.

"You still here, Gavin?"

Startled, he turned his head toward the classroom door and saw John Paul Walker, a fellow teacher. "Yeah, J.P. I'm working on something for tomorrow."

"Don't stay too late," J.P. advised. "If you keep this up, you'll burn out before Christmas." He raised a hand. "See ya."

Gavin waved. When J.P. was gone, he rose and grabbed his suit jacket from the back of his chair. There was someone he needed to see.

By late afternoon, Marcia had memorized all her lines and was working on how she would deliver them. There were several ways to play someone who was about to lose control, and she stood before the mirror in her bathroom playing out variations of the character.

"If that's all, then I must excuse myself, gentlemen," she read. "I have work to do."

There was a faint pounding sound, but Marcia was so involved with her script that she paid no attention. The pounding persisted, and she finally realized it was someone at the door. She dropped her script on the counter and hurried to answer the knock.

"That was a short day," she said happily as she swung the door open, fully expecting to see Jackson, minus his key.

But it was Gavin. He stood with his arm perched against the doorjamb, a faint smile playing on his lips.

"Actually, it was a rather long day," he said, sauntering into her apartment.

Marcia crossed her arms. "I told you I didn't want to see you."

"And I told you that if you didn't agree to see me, I would come to see you."

"This is ridiculous," she muttered. "How did you get up here? We're supposed to have security—" She stopped short when she saw that Gavin was no longer listening to her. He was totally absorbed in studying her from head to toe.

Self-consciously, she rubbed one bare foot on top of the other. She suddenly felt very naked as his eyes drank in every curve and contour of her body.

"Gavin!"

He jerked his gaze from her feet to her eyes. "Yes?"

"Stop looking at me like that."

"I can't help it. You're so beautiful."

He stepped past her into the living room, surveying everything. He strolled over to an African painting and eyed it with interest. He turned to her smiling a strained smile. "Nice place."

"Thank you."

"Did you pick out everything yourself?"

"We both did."

"Jackson, right?"

"Yes."

"I hear he's doing pretty well for himself."

"Like you care about Jackson." She crossed her arms again in a subconsciously defensive gesture. "You know what, I don't need this. I really just want you to leave. Immediately."

"I can't. Not after the nerve it took to come up here. If I leave now—" He shrugged, giving her a look that was sheepish and rueful. And totally disarming.

Marcia's stomach knotted. What was she to do when, each time she saw him, her resolve weakened and she was drawn to him as irresistibly as the first time she met him?

Gavin walked over to an exquisite painting of two swans entwined. Marcia's heart thundered in her chest; she prayed he didn't ask her about the painting.

He asked, "How's the acting going?"

"It's going." She wasn't about to supply him with any more information than that. He had made it clear to her in the past that he did not care about her passion for acting.

"Any big parts?"

"Nothing I'd tell you about."

Gavin raised his hands in surrender. "Okay. I won't go there." He looked into her eyes then, his expression unreadable. Suddenly stepping toward her, he reached out and delicately stroked her cheek.

Her breath caught at the unexpected touch and the warmth that flooded through her body. She stepped back, raising her hands. "Don't touch me!"

"Marcia, I was a fool to let you go."

He closed the distance between them, wrapping his brawny arms around her. She wanted to push him away but couldn't. His eyes held her mesmerized, powerless to move.

"This is just like it used to be," he murmured. "Don't tell me you don't feel anything, Marcia. Not when what I'm feeling is this strong."

"No," she protested weakly. "You're wrong...this is all wrong."

"It's right, Marcia."

His mouth claimed hers, the kiss tender and tentative, probing gently to the very depth of her soul. It was as if her body was completely ignoring her mind. She didn't want to be here, locked in Gavin's embrace, responding to his kiss. She wanted to be far away from him, to never see him again.

Yet her body warmed all over, and her arms slipped around his neck as his kiss became more urgent, his tongue exploring her mouth, his hands caressing her back, her hips. Yes, this was right. It felt so good. The taste and feel of him were as intoxicating as ever. Oh, how she'd missed him!

The thought startled her out of the enchantment. Abruptly, she pushed him away, running the back of her hand over her swollen lips.

"Marcia—" He looked dazed, raw desire burning in his eyes. "I still want you."

"Don't!" Her breath came in quick gasps. "J-Just leave!"

"You don't mean that. You enjoyed the kiss as much as I did. You felt what I felt. Deny it all you want, Marcia, but we belong together."

There was a part of her heart, just a tiny part, that softened at his words—that part of her heart that wished they could have seen their dream realized. Her throat was suddenly very dry, and she swallowed hard to soothe it. It was as if all her breath was getting caught there, refusing to go to her lungs, refusing to let her speak.

But then she remembered the grief he had caused her in the past, and she found her voice once again. "You couldn't be more wrong." She physically pushed him toward the door. "I don't want to see you again, Gavin."

"That's not true." He paused in the doorway. "You responded to me, Marcia. Your kiss didn't lie."

She threw him a stony glance. "I've moved on, Gavin. And you're intruding. This is where I live with Jackson, in case you've forgotten."

"I haven't. But I want you to think about starting over with me."

Incredulous, she stared at him. "Start over? You've got some nerve!"

He gave her a penetrating look, one that probed deep into her heart. She neither flinched nor evaded his gaze but hoped that he would see as little of her most secret feelings as she could see of his at this moment.

"I'm a changed man, Marcia. I've had a lot of time to think about—"

"Good. Use that knowledge in your next relationship," she retorted, her tone sour. "That way, you won't make the same mistakes you did with me. But then, you should be smarter than to get involved with someone who has a mind of her own."

Marcia saw his jaw muscle tighten and knew that her words had hurt him. She felt a twinge of guilt. Maybe that comment hadn't been called for, but as far as she was concerned, it was the truth. Everything had been wonderful between them—blissfully so—until she hadn't done what he expected. When she refused to do his bidding, he walked out on her and never looked back.

And her life would never be the same because of it.

"I'm sorry, Marcia," he said at last "I truly am. I only hope that in time you can forgive me, and we can at least be friends."

She did not trust her voice, and merely gave a noncommittal shrug.

"Goodbye, Marcia."

Gavin turned then, disappearing down the hallway. Marcia quickly closed the door behind him. Releasing the breath she didn't realize she had been holding, she rested her forehead against the door.

She should feel relieved now that he was finally gone. Instead, though, a combination of emotions warred within her—anger, desire, sadness, regret.

If only Gavin would stay out of her life.

But deep inside her heart, she knew she had not seen the last of him.

Six-and-a-half years ago…

"Come here, you." Gavin slipped his arms around her waist and pulled her into his room. This was the first time they had seen each other since making love for the very first time. Gavin's eyes sparkled as he looked down at her, and she felt her knees turn to jelly.

"I missed you."

"But you saw me yesterday."

"Has it been that long?"

Marcia giggled. "It does seem like forever, doesn't it?"

He kissed her then, deeply, mating his tongue with her own. Marcia moaned when he ran his fingers along the length of her spine and cupped her buttocks. She was already hot with desire, and she'd barely been with him two minutes!

With his mouth still on hers, Gavin scooped her up and carried her to the bed, gently easing her down. Marcia closed her eyes, enjoying the feel of his body pressed close to hers, taking in the faint scent of his musky cologne.

She couldn't wait to make love to him for the second time...

Marcia awoke with a start, only to find that she had been dreaming. She glanced at the digital clock on her night table. It read one-twenty-six a.m.

She hugged the fluffy white comforter closely to her body. She'd been dreaming about Gavin—again. Why couldn't she get him out of her system? He had become like a virus she just couldn't shake.

She should be dreaming about her audition, about the lines that Jackson had helped her rehearse earlier.

Instead, every time she closed her eyes, all she could see was Gavin—his sweet smile, his cute dimples, his compelling eyes.

Beside her, Marcia could hear the faint sound of Jackson's breathing as he lay sleeping, and she grimaced. Here she was, in bed with Jackson, yet she was dreaming about Gavin. She felt more than a little guilty about the kiss she had shared with her former lover earlier.

And about the way she had kicked him out.

Marcia groaned miserably as she shifted onto her side.

She was going crazy. That's what her problem was.

Restless, Gavin rolled over onto his side. In a few hours, he had to get up and get ready for work, but he just couldn't sleep. All he could think of was Marcia.

After she kicked him out of her place, he had gone to the gym and run ten laps around the track. Usually, running helped alleviate his stress, but this time it did nothing. As he ran, all he could think about was the kiss he had shared with Marcia, the way her full, soft lips felt against his, the way she had eagerly responded to his touch.

He had gotten carried away, and if she hadn't stopped him, he probably would have swept her off to the bedroom and made sweet, passionate love to her. In a bed she shared with her current boyfriend.

Why did he lose control every time he saw her?

Because he loved her and didn't want to waste any more time being apart from the woman he wanted to share the rest of his life with.

"You should be smarter than to get involved with someone who has a mind of her own..."

Her words stung him as severely as any slap. How could he make her see that he had changed, that he still loved her? He wanted her back in his life. It was as simple as that.

Or not so simple.

Was she really in love with Jackson? If she were, that would certainly pose a greater challenge than he had originally anticipated. His jaw tensed as he thought of Marcia with Jackson, laughing with him, lying in his arms, eating breakfast with him. All the things that he should have been doing with her.

She couldn't be in love with Jackson, Gavin decided. At least not the way she had loved him. Theirs had been a fierce and passionate love, an all-consuming one. They had even been engaged.

He had almost married her.

He pounded a fist into the pillow. It didn't do any good to reminisce over the way things had been; all that was doing was driving him crazy. He needed to concentrate on the future and getting Marcia back.

But he knew now that he mustn't pressure her or come on too strong. If he wanted her back in his life, he would have to first regain her trust. And the only way he could do that was by being her friend.

CHAPTER SEVEN

Wednesday arrived all too soon. As Marcia walked into the casting agent's office, she was amazed at the number of other black females vying for the role of Mary Wiles. No doubt some were reading for other characters, but to see so many contenders still unnerved her.

She rubbed her palms together nervously as she approached the receptionist to sign in. Normally, if she felt good about a part, she didn't care how many others she would be competing with. And she did feel good about this part. She was only worried because she so desperately wanted this role.

Concentrating on the sign-in sheet, Marcia told herself to relax. She knew this particular casting director, Vicki, knew her well and respected her work.

After filling in all the information, she took a seat in the waiting area among the other hopefuls. She didn't join in any conversation but concentrated on her performance, rereading her lines. Occasionally, she looked up to observe the other women. Some were silent like her, mentally concentrating. Others, however, talked nonstop, laughing and giggling. Marcia wondered how they could do it; maybe they only cared about the socializing aspect of an audition. Marcia was here to get the job.

She was called into the casting room ten minutes later. Casting director Vicky introduced her to the film director and producer. Both men sat at a table at the far end of the room.

"Do you want to stand or sit to do this?" Vicki asked.

"Stand." This would allow her the freedom to move around if necessary.

The audition began. Vicki read the lines that didn't belong to Marcia's character. When Marcia finished the scene, she looked at the director and producer, saw them exchange words, then smile at her. They asked her to do it once more, and once again their reaction was the same.

Inwardly, Marcia beamed. This was a good sign, but there were still several other people they had to see.

She left feeling elated. She loved it when she did a good read. A lousy read would have haunted her for the rest of the day and maybe even the next, but when she did a good read, she felt like she was walking on clouds.

She was still elated over her audition when her friend Rachel called her later that evening.

"Hi, Rachel. What's up?"

"I'm waiting, Marcia. I thought you'd be on your way by now. Or are we not going to bother getting a bite to eat first?"

For a moment, Marcia had no idea what Rachel was talking about, then suddenly she remembered. "Oh! The movie!"

"You forgot."

"I'm sorry. I'm on cloud nine over an audition I had earlier, and, well…yes, I did forget. I did forget. We probably have time for a quick bite, I think. I'm on my way. Right now."

Marcia had just picked Rachel up and, as far as Rachel knew, was taking her to see a movie since they hadn't hung out together in quite a long time.

The truth was, Marcia was taking her to Lonita's house for a surprise baby shower.

Rachel was only five months pregnant, and there was no way she would suspect that her friends would throw her a baby shower now. At least that was what her friends were counting on. Rachel was not an easy person to surprise, but this time, Marcia was counting on it.

"Oh darn," Marcia said as convincingly as she could. "I forgot I've got to pick something up at Lonita's. Is that okay?"

Rachel nodded while glancing at her watch. "Sure, we've got time."

Marcia pulled into the driveway of the townhouse where Lonita lived. "Why don't you come in and say hi?" she suggested to Rachel. "I'm sure Lonita would like to see you."

"Knowing how long you might be, maybe I'd better."

Rachel unfastened her seat belt and followed Marcia up the few steps to the door. Marcia knocked three times, and then immediately rang the doorbell. That was her signal to everyone inside that the guest of honor had arrived.

Lonita swung open the door, and Marcia entered the house first. When Rachel followed, her friends suddenly jumped from behind the doors and couches where they had been hiding and yelled, "Surprise!"

Rachel stood, wide-eyed and speechless.

"I think we actually surprised her!" said Lonita, and the crowd began cheering.

Finally, Rachel started to smile, then turned to Marcia and gave her a mock-warning glance. "You are in big trouble, girl."

"It wasn't my idea," Marcia protested.

"Well, then, all of you are in trouble," Rachel said, pointing to everyone in the room. "You know I hate surprises."

"Too bad." Marcia threw her arms around Rachel and hugged her. "It's about time that we got you." She kissed her on the cheek. "Congratulations."

"Thank you."

Marcia kept an arm around Rachel and walked her into the living room. "Now sit."

"Yes, mother," Rachel said in a childlike voice.

The rest of the guests made their way over to Rachel to hug and congratulate her. There were eighteen women total, and within minutes, the house hummed with chatter and laughter. There was a table with finger foods and a bowl of fruit punch for everyone to enjoy.

"So when's the wedding?" one woman asked. Marcia didn't recognize her and assumed that she was one of Rachel's co-workers.

"Yeah," a few others chimed.

Rachel cast them an innocent glance, then shrugged.

"You two are gonna have a baby," Andrea said. "Don't you think it's time you tied the knot?"

Rachel held up a hand to quiet her inquisitive friends. "We're talking about it, and when we figure it out, you all will be the first to know."

There were some suggestive "oohs" throughout the crowd, and everyone laughed again.

Lonita picked up the first present and passed it to Rachel. "Well, girlfriend. This one's from me."

Rachel gave Lonita a fond look before tearing off the wrapping paper. Delighted, she held up a white quilted baby blanket, then reached for Lonita's hand, squeezing it affectionately.

Rachel continued opening her gifts, and when she was done, she had everything from jumpers to shoes to baby bottles. Her eyes glistened with tears as she thanked everyone.

Marcia wasn't sure when it hit her, but seeing all those baby gifts caused her body to flood with an incredible sense of loss. She forced a smile as she fought back tears. She didn't want to feel jealous; Rachel had wanted to get pregnant for a long time and had finally succeeded. That was wonderful, but—

Suddenly, Marcia needed to get away. She rose and went to the bathroom, closing and locking the door behind her. Immediately, the tears came. She gripped the sink for balance as she cried.

Cried for her baby.

The baby no one knew about.

The baby she had lost.

When he was born, she had been elated and immediately forgot about the hours of pain she had endured to deliver him. But she had noticed instantly that something was wrong. She could read it on the nurses' faces.

"Is it a boy or a girl?" she had asked, ignoring the uneasy feeling.

One of the nurses gave her a quick look. "A boy."

They hovered over the baby, doing things Marcia wasn't able to see. Joy turned to bewilderment.

"I want my son," she demanded. "I want to hold him."

"Just try to relax," one nurse said, patting her arm.

"I don't want to relax. I want my son!"

The doctor turned to her. "I'm sorry, Miss Robertson. We did all we could, but your baby was stillborn."

Marcia screamed, "It's a lie! A horrible lie!" She had just given birth; of course her baby was fine. "Give him to me. I want to hold him."

A nurse wrapped the baby in a white blanket, then sadly approached Marcia and gave her the small bundle.

"Oh," Marcia cooed when she saw the tiny dark face. He was perfect. He had a thick patch of hair, and the cutest little nose she had ever seen. He looked like Gavin.

But the baby wouldn't open his eyes.

All around her, the concerned hospital staff watched her. A couple of the nurses were crying.

Marcia touched her son's soft skin. Fear gripped her as she sensed a truth too painful to admit.

The nurse had taken the baby from her, leaving her reaching for him, an unbearable pain overwhelming her.

"No!" she had screamed again. "It's a lie!"

In Lonita's bathroom, Marcia doubled over in pain as she relived her worst nightmare. Losing Gavin had been bad enough, but losing her baby—that had been unbearable.

Someone knocked on the bathroom door, and Marcia fought to gain control.

"Just a minute," she called. She turned on the water faucet and splashed her face with cold water.

When she was composed, she opened the door. Lonita stood outside.

"My God!" Lonita exclaimed. "What's wrong?"

"I'm feeling sick."

Lonita wrapped an arm around Marcia's waist. "Do you want to lie down?"

Marcia shook her head. "No. I…I just want to go."

"You don't look okay to drive."

"I'll be fine." Marcia took a deep breath. "But I need to get home and to bed. Do you think someone else can take Rachel home?"

"Of course. Don't you worry about that."

"Good. Just give me a minute, okay?"

Lonita didn't argue any further. She went into the bathroom, leaving Marcia in the small hallway. Marcia leaned back against the wall and stayed there until she was sure she had herself under control. She was an actress. She could do this.

She walked back into the living room, smiling. "Hey everybody. It's been nice, but I really do have to run."

"Why are you leaving so soon?" Andrea asked.

Hugging her sister, Marcia whispered, "Ask Lonita."

She kissed Rachel. "Congratulations," she told her as enthusiastically as was possible.

When she was finally in her car, she dug her cellular phone out of her purse. Instinctively, she dialed a number that for some reason she had committed to memory. Gavin's number.

After a few seconds, Gavin answered.

At the sound of his voice, Marcia froze. What was she going to say to him? Why had she even called?

Because she needed to know that she wasn't crazy. She needed to know that their love had been real, that their baby had been real.

"Hello?" Gavin said again.

She flipped the phone closed. What on earth was she doing?

Whispering a prayer for strength, she started her car and began to drive. She had to forget Gavin… forget everything. If it was the last thing she did, she was going to put the past behind her.

Once and for all.

CHAPTER EIGHT

"See you Monday, Mr. Williams," one of Gavin's students called as she trotted through the door.

"Don't forget to do your math equations, Emily," he reminded her just before she disappeared. Despite the distance, he heard her groan.

Gavin chuckled. He thoroughly enjoyed teaching. He had known from when he was a child that this profession was going to be his career.

But it wasn't easy. Adapting to life in Japan had been very difficult, but the students were well behaved and eager to learn. The school system was rigid and didn't allow children to learn at their own pace, yet in his classes, he had tried to foster an atmosphere conducive to child-centered learning.

Here, he was much happier with the way he could run his classroom. The principal had been impressed with his immediate rapport with the students, with the way Gavin motivated them to learn. Gavin found children much more willing to learn if they knew their destinies were in their own hands, and if their assessment wasn't based only on pen-and-paper tests. There were many other ways children could show that they were learning, that they were achieving success, and that was one of the things Gavin loved about his job. That, and the fact that he got to work with children all day.

His mind wandered to Marcia as it had every day this week. If they had still been together, they would have most likely had a child or two by now.

The memory was bittersweet. Marcia and Gavin had talked about having at least two children. If they had a boy, they would name him Marcus Anthony—after Gavin's brother and Marcia's father. They hadn't decided on a name for a little girl, but Marcia had been partial to Nicola.

The memory was so clear to Gavin it seemed like yesterday. He wished he could be going home to Marcia and a couple of children instead of only dreaming about it.

"Do you want to go to dinner tonight?"

Gavin looked up to see J.P. standing in the doorway.

"If you want, we can even get some planning done."

"How about dinner and a few drinks?" Gavin suggested. "No more planning for this week. I'm already burned out."

J.P. smiled. "Sure. Sounds good to me."

It sounded great to Gavin. This was just the distraction he needed. Tonight was one night he did not want to be home alone dreaming of Marcia.

He grabbed his briefcase and his jacket. "Let's go."

Marcia didn't know how she made it through the week. Rachel's baby shower had depressed her more than she anticipated, and with Jackson working late into the nights, she had too much time to think of the baby she had lost.

To ease the pain, Marcia worked out vigorously in the building's gym and read. That helped somewhat to take her mind off the tormenting past. And when Jackson came home from work, she clung to him for comfort.

She had never told Jackson about her pregnancy. Nobody knew. When he asked her why she seemed so down, she told him that she was worried about the audition, about whether or not she would get the role. That was partly the truth, but it wasn't what made her depressed.

Marcia was thrilled when her agent finally called and told her that the part of the lawyer was hers. The good news was exactly what she needed to cheer herself up. She needed to concentrate on work. And she needed to share the good news with Jackson.

He usually went out for a drink with the other actors on Friday nights, but he always called her first. Tonight, she would tell him to forget going out. She had a surprise, a celebration.

She rushed out to the mall and bought incense and fresh candles as well as wine. She wanted the night to be special for her and Jackson.

She needed it to be special.

Shortly after seven o'clock, the phone rang. Anxious, Marcia answered it. "Jackson?"

"It's Andrea."

"Oh, hi." Marcia settled onto the love seat. "How are you?"

"It's over with Curtis."

"It is?" Marcia asked skeptically. "Are you sure about that?"

"This time, I'm definitely sure."

"What happened to bring you to your senses?"

"It was just the same-old, same-old, and I decided that I'd had enough."

"Don't tell me—" Marcia began, trying to deduce the actual meaning of Andrea's words. "He's married?"

"He's living with someone," Andrea said glumly.

Big surprise, Marcia thought. "Good for you. I mean, good for you that you decided to leave him.

And please kick him to the curb when he comes crying back to you."

"This time it's for good," Andrea explained. "And Lonita and I are going out tonight to celebrate. Want to come along?"

Marcia hesitated, considering her sister's offer.

"I thought that you of all people would be thrilled to learn that I had finally dumped Curtis," Andrea added.

"Oh, I am," Marcia stressed. "It's just that I have some good news of my own, and I was planning to stay home and celebrate."

"What kind of news?"

"I got the part in that film I was telling you about."

Andrea squealed with delight. "You did?"

"Sure did!"

"That's even more reason for you to come out with us tonight and celebrate."

"Actually, I was planning to surprise Jackson with a romantic evening."

Andrea paused for a moment, then said, "Oh. I guess there's no way to talk you out of that?"

"Not tonight. But what about tomorrow? I'm all for that."

Reluctantly, Andrea agreed. After all, she didn't have a choice. Marcia wouldn't change her mind about going out that evening. She needed to be with Jackson.

J.P. waved a hand in front of Gavin's eyes. "Earth to Gavin."

Gavin snapped out of his trance. "I'm sorry."

The two men were at a small sports bar in the west side of the city. They'd had dinner first at a steak house, then had come here to watch a football game and have a few beers.

"Don't tell me you're still thinking about work," J.P. admonished. "Because you're the one who said to forget about work for tonight."

"I only wish I were thinking about work."

J.P. cast him a skeptical glance. "If not work, what then?"

"You don't want to know."

J.P. rolled his eyes. "If it's not work, then it's got to be a woman."

"Damn, is it that obvious?"

J.P. nodded. "Is this someone you're dating, or would like to date?"

"Someone," Gavin responded slowly, "I used to date."

J.P. settled back in his chair. "What happened?"

"We broke up."

J.P. rolled his eyes again. "I figured that much. What's the story?"

"The story is—I was a jerk. I was young and stupid and in love, and I ruined everything."

"Uh-huh."

"After the breakup, I had to get away. I went to Japan to teach English for three years."

"Did it help?"

"I was sure I was over her. I mean, I still thought about her, but I was too busy to think of her constantly, like I'm doing now."

J.P. took a long draft of his beer. "So what's different now?"

"I guess being back in Toronto. So many blasted memories that I can't stop thinking about her."

"Obviously you're still in love. Have you told her?"

"I've talked to her." Gavin shrugged with assumed nonchalance. "But she doesn't want to have anything to do with me."

"Ouch."

"And she has a boyfriend. She's living with him."

"Double ouch."

"Normally, if she were another girl, I would just forget her. But I can't." Gavin downed the dregs of his beer. "Did I mention that we were engaged?"

J.P. gave Gavin a pitying look. "You were engaged, you blew it, and now you want her back, but she wants nothing to do with you, and there's this other guy. That's a tough break. Let me buy you another beer."

"To drown my sorrows?" Gavin grimaced wryly. "I haven't given up, my friend."

"Hey, go for it."

Gavin rose. "Give me a minute. I'm going to the washroom."

When Gavin was out of J.P.'s sight, he made his way to the pay telephones. His cell phone was in the car, but he wasn't about to go get it. He fished in his pocket for a quarter, then plopped it into the slot. He dialed the number to Marcia's condo.

She answered the phone on the first ring. "Hi." By her tone, it was clear to Gavin that she had been expecting someone other than him. Probably Jackson.

"Hello, Marcia."

"Gavin?"

"Yeah, it's me."

She paused for several moments before saying anything. "How are you?"

"I'm okay. How are you?"

"Actually," she said happily, "I'm very well. I just found out that I got a part that I auditioned for."

"Really?" Gavin asked. "That's great."

Marcia paused once more. "Sorry, I forgot. That's not something that would interest you."

"No," Gavin said quickly. "You're wrong. I'm very happy for you, and I wish you great success in your career."

Again there was silence. She finally said, "I hope you mean that Gavin."

"I do. I've already told you that there are a lot of things I regret about the past."

"Gavin—"

"Don't worry," he said quickly. "That's not why I called. I just called…I just called to let you know that I am thinking about you."

Marcia did not respond, and Gavin held the phone to his ear, at a loss for words. He finally asked softly, "Did you hear me?"

"Yes, I heard you."

He didn't want to push her. And he certainly didn't expect her to jump for joy when he called her. He did, however, want her to get the point that he still cared for her and wasn't going to go away.

"I won't keep you, Marcia," he finally said. "I just wanted to call and tell you that. Enjoy your evening."

Marcia held the receiver to her chest for several minutes after Gavin hung up. The moment she had heard his voice, she had been mentally preparing for a battle.

She hadn't expected Gavin to say that he was thinking of her. It was something he used to do when they were dating. He would call her sometimes and just say, "I'm thinking of you," and hang up, leaving Marcia glowing all over.

When she had heard him say the words, her heart had started beating with excitement. It angered her that he still could affect her like this, that simple words from him could have her tingling all over.

Was it this hard for others to get over their first love? Maybe it was because he was her first love that she was having so much trouble forgetting him. Their love had been wonderful—for a moment in time.

Marcia looked at the clock. It was almost eight. With any luck, Jackson would be coming home soon.

She pushed all thoughts of Gavin to the back of her mind. She had to get everything ready for her romantic evening with Jackson.

CHAPTER NINE

Lonita and Andrea moved through the dense crowd at The Palace. "Too bad Marcia couldn't come out with us," Andrea commented.

"You didn't expect her to choose us over a romantic evening with Jackson?" Lonita spied a bit of space near the dance floor and pulled Andrea toward it. "But I'm glad we're here. The men sure are looking good tonight."

"And so are we." Andrea grinned at her friend, sensational in a white tank top and a short leather skirt with low-cut boots.

Andrea was dressed in a classic black form-fitting dress and looked like a million bucks. She was ready to prove that she was over Curtis, and what better way than to get out and meet other men. Her eyes followed a gorgeous man squeezing by. He didn't notice her. But there was always later.

Two men approached them, smiling. Lonita rolled her eyes. They were not the most attractive pair in the crowd.

"Ladies," one of the men said enthusiastically. "How are you doing tonight?"

"Up until now, we were doing just fine," Andrea blurted out.

Lonita couldn't help but giggle. She loved Andrea, especially her brashness.

"Well, maybe we can buy you a drink and make things better," the second man suggested.

Lonita and Andrea exchanged glances; these two had totally missed the point.

"How about that drink?" the second man prodded.

Lonita looked at Andrea and shrugged. A drink was a drink as far as she was concerned, and she didn't care who was buying it.

Marcia lit the last candle in the living room, then backed up to observe her creation. She'd lit twelve candles and placed them on the coffee table, the end tables, and the windowsill.

She smiled. The room looked beautiful. She'd just had the sudden impulse to be romantic—and the candlelight setting had worked well before.

Marcia looked down at what she was wearing and realized that it was completely inappropriate. A pink T-shirt and gray sweat pants were hardly romantic. She wanted to look beautiful—irresistible—for Jackson.

She went to the bedroom, where the digital clock read nine-thirty-eight. She showered in five minutes, then creamed her body with a perfume-scented lotion. She slipped into a black lace camisole, one that didn't hide a single glimpse of her best assets. Looking at herself in the mirror, she said, "Jackson, I'm gonna have no mercy with you tonight."

Lonita stood resting her left elbow on the bar, a piña colada in her right hand. Andrea had ordered a beer. The cold bar rail dug into their backs, but if they shifted so much as an inch, they'd be pressed against their two suitors, who stood directly in front of them, leaving hardly any breathing space at all.

The DJ started playing a slow song. Andrea finished her drink, then discreetly nudged Lonita, urging her to do the same.

"How about a dance?" one of the men asked Andrea.

"Actually," Andrea began, "I've got to go to the washroom." She linked arms with Lonita. "Come on."

Lonita shrugged as she looked at the men. "We'll be right back."

"We'll be right here," the second one said. His eyes roamed her body like an unwanted caress.

Andrea dragged Lonita until they were in the safety of the washroom. Once there, Andrea made a face. "I refuse to spend the rest of the night talking to those two losers."

"Ditto. Let's hang out in here until the slow jams finish."

Andrea looked around and surveyed the crowd of women that had filtered into the washroom. "I think they all are doing the same thing we're doing."

"There must be a lot of losers out there."

A woman brushed past Andrea on her way to the mirror, stepping on her foot, but she didn't even bother to apologize. Andrea shot her an annoyed look, then said to Lonita, "I've changed my mind. Let's go back out and find ourselves some real men."

Lonita nodded her agreement, then followed Andrea as she led the way out of the washroom. They walked in the opposite direction of the bar, and, thankfully for them the club was large and there were lots of places to disappear.

"Oh, look," Andrea said, pointing. "I think that's the guy I saw when we first got here. Let's go say hi."

Andrea and Lonita maneuvered their way through the crowd toward the object of Andrea's desire. When they were about five feet away from him, Lonita yanked Andrea's hand, bringing her to a stop.

"Lonita!" Andrea protested. "What are you—"

"Look who's here," Lonita said, cutting her off.

"Who?"

"Over there." Lonita pointed in the direction of the dance floor.

"Oh my goodness," Andrea said, as she found the "who" Lonita was talking about.

It was Jackson.

After half-an-hour of lying provocatively on the sofa, Marcia got up and stretched her legs. If Jackson didn't get home soon, she would probably fall asleep.

She decided to open the bottle of wine and have it ready with two glasses for Jackson's arrival.

Again, she looked at the clock, but it only confirmed what she already knew. It was late, and given the time Jackson had started work this morning, he should have been home by now.

Marcia turned on the living room lights and looked for the phone number for the set of *The Beat*. It was a cell phone number, and if they were still shooting, someone would answer it.

The number rang and rang. Marcia hung up and tried again. Still, there was no answer.

They probably just wrapped, Marcia told herself, hoping she was right. If that was the case, then Jackson would surely be home within the next thirty to forty minutes.

Marcia turned on the CD player and began playing a Brian McKnight CD. This would help her pass the time until Jackson came home. It would also provide wonderful background music as they made love.

Jackson was dancing with a white woman, a blonde, with very large breasts.

"What's he doing with her?" Lonita asked.

"Why isn't he home with Marcia?" Andrea retorted bitterly.

The two watched Jackson dance. He was much taller than the girl and had to bend to bring his head close to hers. Her hands were clasped tightly around his neck, pulling him close. Jackson's hands were wrapped around her small waist. As Andrea and Lonita watched, his hands ventured down, cupping the blonde's buttocks, then squeezing them provocatively.

"Oh, brother," Andrea said.

"What a dog."

The two continued to watch Jackson in fascinated horror, unable to fathom the cold, hard, reality. When the songs changed from slow to funky, Jackson and the girl remained together, winding and grinding their body parts.

"That man has some nerve to do this to my sister," Andrea said angrily. "I'm gonna go over there and give him a piece of my mind."

"No, don't," Lonita said, grabbing her arm. "If you go over there now, he'll just deny everything. We have to stay quiet and watch him, then tell Marcia everything we saw."

Jackson and the blonde wove through the crowd on the dance floor until they reached a clear spot near the wall. Andrea and Lonita had to reposition themselves to get a closer look, and when they did, they got an eyeful.

Jackson pressed against the blonde, and he had her cornered against the wall. His hands roaming all over her curvaceous body, he bent his head and kissed her.

A long kiss.

An urgent kiss.

The blonde wrapped one of her legs around Jackson's as they continued to embrace each other, as they continued to lock lips.

"This is making me sick," said Andrea and turned away.

Lonita shook her head, disgusted. "I can't believe that jerk."

Jackson and the blonde must have realized that they were getting a little too hot and heavy in public, because when Andrea looked again, the two pulled apart, then walked arm-in-arm toward the club's exit.

"He's gonna leave with her," Andrea said, seething. "I can't believe it. Jackson is cheating on my sister!"

Hours later, Marcia was fast asleep in the bedroom and didn't hear when Jackson entered.

Quietly, he stripped out of his clothes and climbed into bed next to her.

She stirred, waking up slowly. Instantly, she realized that she was not alone in the bed. She stretched to turn on the bedside lamp, then turned to face Jackson.

"Hi," he said softly.

"Hi? That's all you're going to say?"

"I'm sorry," he added. "I know I should have called, but I just got caught up with the guys, and before I knew it, I'd had a few drinks. Then I noticed how late it was and figured you'd be sleeping."

Marcia gave him a skeptical look. "I was waiting all night."

"I'm sorry."

"I had a special evening planned."

Jackson raised himself on one elbow. "What kind of evening?"

"Wine, candlelight."

"Oh, don't tell me that."

"A brand new negligee."

Jackson leaned closer. "What color?"

Marcia shrugged. "It was no big deal. Black. See-through."

Jackson wrapped his arms around her. He kissed her throat, her cheek, her ear, then whispered, "Why don't you go try it on?"

Marcia pulled back and placed a hand on Jackson's chest to keep him at bay. "Not so fast. I'm not in the mood anymore."

"I can fix that."

Her reply was sharp. "No."

"Marcia, I'm sorry I spoiled your plans. But I'm here now."

"It's not that simple, Jackson. I had some news I wanted to share with you...you didn't even call."

"I've explained why."

"Yeah, well, you never used to forget to call. You never used to party so much."

"I always go out with the guys on Friday night. You know that."

"And now you're staying out later and later, and not calling..." Marcia turned off the bedside lamp, then sank back against the pillow. "Forget it. Good night, Jackson."

"No, let's work this out. You're right. I should have called. I should have shown more consideration. In the future, I promise to call, even if it's late."

He slipped an arm around her, but she didn't respond.

"And I know you're upset because we don't spend much time together anymore, so I promise to make more time for us. Will that make you happy?"

Marcia remained silent. She wasn't going to make this easy for him.

"Oh, come on, baby. You know you mean everything to me, even if I don't always show it. How can I make this up to you? Name your price."

"I can't be bought."

"But you can be pampered. How about it? Do you have plans tomorrow?"

"No."

"Then tomorrow will be your day. And believe me, I'll make it one you won't forget."

CHAPTER TEN

Andrea heaved a restless sigh, then dropped herself onto the sofa in Lonita's living room. "Try her again. Maybe she's just not answering."

"I've already tried five times." Lonita chewed on a fingernail as she paced anxiously. "Maybe she's just not in."

Andrea marched over to the phone and picked up the receiver. She started dialing.

Lonita rolled her eyes. "Oh, so you've got the magic touch, do you?"

Andrea ignored her as she dialed. Marcia often let the answering machine pick up if she didn't want to be bothered. But Andrea desperately needed to reach her. She couldn't stand the thought of Jackson being with her sister even one more day.

When Jackson and Marcia's answering machine came on, Andrea said, "Marcia, pick up. Come on, girl. I need to talk to you. It's Andrea!" She frowned when Marcia did not pick up. "Okay. Just give me a call as soon as you get this message."

She hung up the phone with a resounding thud, then turned to face Lonita. "I guess she's not home."

"Really? Now what gave you that idea?"

Marcia clutched Jackson's hand tightly and buried her face in his jacket as the elevator soared to the top of the CN Tower. The elevator in this, once the world's tallest building, was made of glass, giving its occupants a clear view of the lake, the expressway, and the buildings below. The speed of ascent made Marcia's stomach queasy, and the view definitely scared her. She clung to Jackson until the elevator came to a stop.

This was the finale to a gloriously romantic day. Jackson was trying to make up for last night, and he certainly was doing it in grand style.

First, he had taken Marcia out sailing on Lake Ontario. Next, they had gone to the city's Harbourfront, where they enjoyed an afternoon jazz festival. After that, while the sun set, they walked along the beach hand-in-hand, simply enjoying each other's company. It had been just the way it was when they had begun courting.

And now, after a quick shower and change, they were going to dine at the fabulous revolving restaurant atop the tower.

Marcia smiled, fondly remembering the day's events as the hostess led them to a table. When

Jackson had told her that today would be her day, she hadn't expected anything this romantic.

Unexpectedly, her mind drifted to Gavin. Gavin had always been romantic. Things like walks on the beach and picnics in the park were second nature to him.

Jackson wasn't the most romantic guy, but when he made an effort, he pulled out all the stops. Marcia couldn't ask for more than that.

Besides, look what had happened between her and Gavin. Stability was much more important than romance, she reflected.

"Marcia?"

Realizing that she had been lost in her thoughts, Marcia lifted her eyes to Jackson and smiled.

"Everything okay?"

She nodded. "Wonderful. Thank you for today."

Jackson brought her hand to his mouth and kissed it. "It's not over yet."

The moment was interrupted by their waitress, an attractive woman with dark hair. "Hello," she began cheerfully. "My name is Margaret, and I'm your server tonight. The special this evening is glazed chicken in an orange and pineapple sauce. It comes with rice, potato or fries, as well as a salad."

"I haven't even looked at the menu," Marcia confessed.

"That's okay," Margaret said. "I'll get your drinks first. Can I tempt you with one of our frozen strawberry daiquiris?"

"I'd like a bottle of your best champagne," Jackson replied.

"Oooh," the waitress chimed. "A special occasion?"

Jackson's eyes were on Marcia as he said simply, "Yes."

Margaret grinned. "I'll be right back."

When Margaret disappeared, Marcia took Jackson's hand in hers. He looked extremely handsome in an olive green suit and matching tie, an outfit that went well with her knee-length violet dress with matching shoulder wrap.

"Thank you, Jackson. You're really spoiling me today."

"You deserve it. Congratulations again on landing that role."

"Thanks. This...what you've done for me today...means so much."

Margaret returned with two glasses, an ice-filled wine cooler, and a bottle of champagne. She popped the cork, then poured a little of the bubbly liquid into Jackson's glass. He took a sip, then nodded his acceptance of the bottle. Margaret filled both their glasses.

"We rarely have people order our best champagne," Margaret said. "The bartender was very excited."

Marcia threw a surreptitious glance at the woman, hoping she wasn't one of those waitresses who spent most of her time talking to her customers. Hopefully she would realize that Marcia and Jackson wanted to spend a quiet evening together.

"Have you had a chance to look over the menu yet?" Margaret asked.

"I'll have the special," Jackson responded.

Marcia flipped open the menu and quickly reviewed its contents. "How's the chicken stir-fry?"

"Oh, that's delicious," was Margaret's reply.

Marcia doubted if she would have said otherwise. "Okay. I'll try that."

Margaret took their menus, casting a lingering glance at Jackson before she left the table. Marcia had learned to ignore the looks other women gave him. After all, he was an attractive man.

"To us," said Jackson.

Marcia touched her glass to his. "I'll drink to that."

She sipped the champagne, the delightful flavor dancing on her tongue. She smiled at Jackson, but he was no longer looking at her. Following his line of sight, she saw what he was looking at, and her euphoric mood dropped.

He was watching the hostess, who was bent over clearing off a table. The short skirt she wore held her butt snugly, and Jackson was apparently enjoying the view.

Annoyed, Marcia cleared her throat...loudly.

Startled back to reality, Jackson returned his attention to Marcia, then took her hand in his. "I've got a surprise for you."

Marcia was about to reprimand him for his lack of consideration, but thought better of it. Jackson was a man after all, and just because he was dating her didn't mean he was dead. "What kind of surprise?"

"The kind you'll like."

He reached into his jacket pocket and extracted a small blue velvet jewelry box. Marcia's eyes lit up, and she threw a hand to her mouth. "Jackson!"

He handed her the box. "Open it."

Marcia was too excited for words. She knew what was in the box, and she could almost cry. Had Jackson had this evening planned before last night? Holding her breath, she opened the small box.

Her heightened excitement over what she was expecting fizzled when she saw what was actually inside. Instead of a diamond engagement ring, the box contained a pair of earrings.

"What—you don't like them?" Jackson asked, obviously sensing her disappointment.

"No. That's not it." She chuckled, somewhat embarrassed. "Of course I love it. They're beautiful."

"They're diamonds," Jackson told her, his eyes probing hers for a response.

"Diamonds?" she asked, delighted. She took one of the dangling pear-shaped earrings out of the box and observed it closely. "Jackson, these are stunning. But...why?"

"Consider it a gift for landing that part."

Marcia was about to respond when she felt someone's presence and turned to see who it was. It was Margaret, hovering over her shoulder.

"Oh, those are gorgeous!" Margaret exclaimed.

"Thank you," Marcia replied dryly.

"You certainly have good taste," Margaret said to Jackson as she placed their salads on the table.

Marcia picked up her fork and was about to partake of her salad when she noticed that Margaret was still standing there. She looked up at the waitress, eyeing her with a quizzical expression.

"Oh, I'm sorry," Margaret said. "It's just that—gosh, I hope you don't mind me asking you this." She was talking to Jackson. "Are you that guy from that show, *The Beat*?"

Smiling widely, Jackson nodded. "Yes. That's me."

"My goodness!" Margaret threw a hand to her chest. "I thought it was you, but I just wasn't sure."

Great, Marcia thought. *Now we'll never be rid of her.*

Jackson continued to smile. "Well, you were right."

Margaret sighed with glee. "I'm just so honored to be serving you." She giggled. "I know you might think this is silly of me, but can I have your autograph?"

Jackson didn't hesitate. "Certainly, Margaret."

"Oh, my goodness." Margaret passed him her notepad to write on. "I can't wait to tell my friend Barbara. She just loves the show."

As Marcia feared, Margaret's commotion got the attention of other patrons in the restaurant, and before she knew it, the table was surrounded by autograph seekers. Obligingly, Jackson signed autographs for everyone who requested them, pausing a few times to smile apologetically at Marcia. By the time they finished dessert, even the manager and the head cook had come out to say hi.

So much for an intimate dinner with the man she loved.

When they returned to the condo, Jackson didn't hesitate to take her in his arms as they stepped through the door. He pulled her against his body and captured her lips with his, kissing her urgently, causing the fire within her to burn out of control. He carried her to bed and wasted no time taking off her dress. When he saw that she was wearing only thong underwear, he moaned.

Marcia loved his reaction to her body.

He was forceful and he was gentle. He was exciting and he was beguiling. And when he had finished loving her, Marcia was left panting, reveling in her body's sweet sensations.

She gripped his back as he quivered, succumbing to his own release. She felt wonderful, and if Jackson continued to love her like this, she would no longer have to feel troubled by Gavin's reappearance in her life.

Gavin. Why on earth had he come into her thoughts when she was making love with Jackson?

There was something wrong with her, something terribly wrong. She had jumped off the deep end and straight into a pool of insanity. Why else would she think of Gavin at a moment like this, when all she wanted was to forget they had ever been lovers?

"Something the matter?" Jackson asked.

Marcia looked into his eyes. "Hold me, Jackson." She snuggled against him. "Hold me tight."

CHAPTER ELEVEN

Marcia watched Jackson as he slept. She was happy, wasn't she? She'd had her doubts about her relationship with Jackson, but after the previous day and night of romance and passion, she knew they were unfounded.

He was in love with her.

And she with him. That she had thought of Gavin while making love with Jackson had been a brief lapse of sanity. It would never happen again.

Jackson opened his eyes and immediately reached for her. His kiss kindled fresh desire, but he broke the kiss with a groan. "I've got to go to the studio."

"The studio? On a Sunday?"

"We're shooting promos for the show." He climbed out of bed. "I told you about that, remember?"

"When will you be back?"

Jackson shrugged. "You know how these sets go."

Unfortunately, Marcia did know how sets went. You never knew when you were finished until you were finished. Well, she couldn't have Jackson to herself all the time. And yesterday certainly had been wonderful enough to tide her over for a while.

Marcia was eating a late breakfast when the phone rang. She answered it on the third ring. "Hello?"

"You're home!" Andrea cried dramatically. "You had us worried sick!"

"Hold up," Marcia said, not yet ready to face her sister's wrath. "What's going on?"

"What's going on is that we called you a thousand times yesterday and left you a thousand messages."

"I was out." Marcia smiled, remembering. "With Jackson."

"All day?"

"Yes, all day. What's so important?"

"There's something that you really need to know. And I mean really."

Marcia was curious, but not ready to deal with Andrea and another one of her crises. "Look, if this is about Curtis—"

"It's not," Andrea responded quickly. "It's about Jackson, and...look, you just need to get your butt over to Lonita's right away. I'm on my way there."

"Why? What's wrong?"

"I can only say that you're not going to like it."

"We think Jackson is having an affair." Although Lonita's expression was troubled as she sat with her friends at the round kitchen table, her voice was clear and calm.

"What?" Marcia asked, staring at her friend and her sister as though they had come from another planet. "What did you say?"

"I said, we think Jackson is having an affair."

Marcia shook her head. "That's absolutely ludicrous. You're dead wrong."

Lonita rested her elbows on the table. "I don't think so. Andrea and I were out at The Palace Friday night, and we saw him. And he was with someone else. A woman."

Marcia shrugged. "So he's got female friends. I've got male friends. That's no big deal."

"They were more than friendly," said Andrea.

"And how would you know?"

"Trust us." Lonita pursed her lips. "We know what we saw. We were both there."

Marcia shook her head in disbelief. "Jackson's a celebrity now. He's bound to have women trying to talk to him. And he knows a lot of people."

"Marcia," Lonita began, her tone gentle, "do you think I would ever do anything to hurt you? You're my dearest friend. And I'm telling you this because I love you."

Marcia smiled at her friend, then reached across the table and squeezed her hand affectionately. "I know that. I'm not suggesting you're making this up to hurt me. It's just that you misinterpreted what you saw—"

"We didn't." Andrea pushed back her chair and stood. "Believe me, I should know."

Marcia looked up at her sister and carefully considered her words before speaking. "Your situation is completely different. Curtis—well, he always was a dog. You just didn't want to face that. Jackson…no, I just can't picture it. He's never been like that. We had such a wonderful day yesterday."

"How nice," Andrea quipped. "I guess the guy has stamina."

Marcia shot her sister an irritated glance. "Excuse me?"

Lonita placed a hand on Marcia's arm. "We wouldn't be telling you this if it weren't true."

Marcia linked her hands behind her neck. "This is why you wanted to see me so urgently?"

Lonita frowned. "Did Jackson tell you where he was on Friday night? The night you were planning that special evening for him?"

"Yeah," Marcia said, nodding. "He went out for a drink after work. He usually does on Fridays. I always know where he is and what he's doing."

As Andrea reclaimed her seat, she asked, "Always?"

"You know what I mean. The point is, I know I can trust him."

"Oh, Marcia," Lonita began sadly, "look at what happened to me. Can we ever really trust anybody else?"

Marcia closed her eyes and let out a ragged breath, frustrated. "Are you even sure it was him? It's hard to see someone in a dark club."

"Marcia," Andrea said frankly, "we were five feet away from him. And the whole time, he was occupied—and I mean occupied—with some girl—some blonde."

Now Marcia was convinced that they had misinterpreted what they saw. "If you were five feet away from him, then there's no way—even if he wanted to—that Jackson would have carried on like that with my sister and my best friend there."

"I don't think he saw us," Lonita said. "Hell, if he did, then that was real brazen. But, Marcia, we saw him kissing her!"

Snatching her purse, Marcia rose from the table. This conversation had passed ridiculous. "Goodbye. I've got things to do."

Exchanging frustrated glances, Lonita and Andrea followed her to the door. Marcia hugged them both. "I know you care about me, and I know what you think you saw. But I know Jackson He wouldn't hurt me like that."

"Then why don't you speak to him," Lonita suggested. "Ask him who he was with and see what he tells you. Because we saw him with some blonde woman with large breasts."

Some blonde woman with large breasts. Lonita's words haunted Marcia all the way home. Jackson had been talking with a blonde at the Film Festival party, and she had been very touchy-feely with him. At the time, she hadn't really thought anything of it. But now...

Now, she needed to see him. To be reassured.

Jackson wasn't there when she got in; no doubt he was still working on the set.

Or was he?

Marcia went over to the phone in the living room, picked up the receiver, and punched in the digits to Jackson's pager. She hung up and waited for his response.

Fifteen minutes passed, and no call. She paged him again.

Her stomach twisted into a tangled knot. Could Lonita and Andrea be right? Was Jackson fooling around? No, that was impossible. She would have suspected something.

Finally, the phone rang. Marcia grabbed it. "Jackson?"

"Yeah, it's me. What's going on?"

"Where are you?"

He paused before answering. “I’m still on the set. Why?”

“I just remembered that I promised my parents we’d go there for dinner tonight.”

“You did? Well, we can do that. It’s still early.”

“It’s not that early,” Marcia said quickly. Her heart was beating erratically. She wanted Jackson to come home as soon as possible. The sooner he did, the sooner she could straighten out this situation. “It’s four o’clock, and I told my mother we’d be there at five.”

“I’m sure she won’t mind if we get there an hour late.”

“When do you think you’ll finish?”

“I don’t know, Marcia. But I don’t think it will be that much longer.”

“Good,” she said. “Get home as soon as you can.”

“Hi, Mom. Dad.” Marcia hugged and kissed her parents. “Hope we’re not too late.”

“Dinner’s been ready for an hour,” her mother said.

“It’s my fault, Mrs. Robertson,” Jackson explained. “I got caught up at work.”

“Oh, don’t you worry. You’re here now. That’s what’s important.” Mrs. Robertson led the way to the dining room.

When they were seated, Marcia asked, "Where's Dwayne?"

A frustrated look crossed Mrs. Robertson's face. "You know your brother. He can't stay at home. He's out with his friends somewhere."

Mr. Robertson frowned. "I only hope he's not in any trouble."

Marcia, too, was worried about her sixteen-year-old brother. He was a smart kid, but he was impressionable, and lately he was keeping company with a rough crowd. He thought he knew everything and didn't want to listen to anybody.

"Dwayne will be just fine," she said to her parents, not wanting them to worry unnecessarily. "He always is."

Mrs. Robertson had prepared West Indian-style chicken, curried goat, a tossed salad, and steamed vegetables. Marcia always looked forward to her mother's meals, but this evening she hardly tasted the food, preoccupied as she was with the tale Andrea and Lonita had told.

When she finished eating, she dropped her hands into her lap and announced, "That was absolutely delicious."

Mrs. Robertson gave her daughter a quizzical look.

"It was, Mom. I hope there's enough for me to take some home."

Mr. Robertson shook his head. "Still haven't learned to cook like your mother, eh?"

"She's getting there." Jackson rubbed the back of Marcia's neck. "But I rarely get to eat one of her meals because I always eat on the set."

"How is the show going?" Mr. Robertson asked.

"Great. I'm working long hours, but I can't complain because I love what I'm doing."

"I watch the show every Friday," said Mr. Robertson.

Jackson grinned. "And what do you think—honestly."

"I like it. It's a bit implausible at times, but then isn't all television?"

Mrs. Robertson stood and smoothed her pink floral skirt, then cleared the plates from the table. "Marcia, why don't you help me with the dessert?"

In the kitchen, Marcia asked, "Where is it?"

"Forget the dessert." Mrs. Robertson placed the dirty dishes in the sink. She turned and looked Marcia squarely in the eye. "Why don't you tell me what's going on."

Marcia was caught completely off guard. "Going on...what do you mean?"

"You're my baby, and a mother knows her baby." She took a few steps toward Marcia, closing the gap between them. She wrapped an arm around her daughter's shoulder. "What's the matter?"

"Nothing, Mom."

"Then you're doing a great job looking like you have a problem."

"Is it that obvious?"

"Probably only to me. Is it Jackson?"

"You could say that."

Mrs. Robertson squeezed Marcia tightly. "You're not ready to talk about it, huh?"

Marcia shook her head. "Not yet. I have to talk to Jackson first."

Mrs. Robertson gave her daughter a sympathetic look. "Well, you better help me with that dessert. Get the plates."

They ate cherry cheesecake in the living room and talked for a little while longer before Jackson announced that he had to work early the next morning, so they had better leave. Marcia kissed her parents goodbye and promised that she would see them soon.

She waited until they were in the car and Jackson had driven awhile before she spoke.

"Jackson, I have to ask you something."

"What?"

Marcia swallowed hard. She wanted to find a way to word her question so that she wouldn't sound accusatory.

"What did you do Friday night?"

"Friday night?"

"Yeah."

"I told you. I went out with some of the guys from work—like always."

"And where did you go?"

Jackson turned his head. "Why are you asking?"

"Can't I ask?"

"Yeah…but is there a point to this?"

"I'll tell you in a minute."

Jackson scowled at the car in front of them. "I went to The Palace. Satisfied?"

"And who were you out with?"

"I already told you."

"No, you didn't."

"Why all the questions?" he asked, beginning to sound annoyed.

"Why do you have a problem answering me?" Marcia challenged.

"I'm not the one with the problem here."

"Then why can't you tell me who you were with?"

"Ashton and Paul. Okay?"

Marcia's heart sank. Andrea and Lonita had been certain when they said they saw Jackson. But they hadn't seen him with his male friends.

"Were you with anyone else?"

"I just told you who I was with," Jackson snapped. "I'm not telling you again."

"Why are you getting so angry?"

"Because I don't like what you're implying."

"And what am I implying?"

"That I'm lying to you."

Marcia took a deep breath, then exhaled slowly. She didn't like the way Jackson was reacting to what she considered simple questions. If he had nothing to hide, he should try to put her mind at ease instead of getting angry with her.

"Who is she, Jackson?"

He gave her a quick, angry glare. "Who is who?"

"The blonde."

"I don't know who you're talking about."

"I'll bet."

Marcia felt the car swerve, and the next thing she knew, Jackson was pulling into a mall parking lot.

"What's this all about, Marcia?"

She did not look at him. "This is about the fact that you lied to me. Lonita and my sister saw you Friday night."

A heavy silence followed her words. Slowly, she turned to face him. "Apparently, you didn't see them because you were too 'occupied' with some blonde."

Still, he said nothing, only gripped the steering wheel.

"Is she the same one from the festival party?"

"No, she isn't." He let go of the steering wheel. "You're blowing this way out of proportion, Marcia."

"Then who is she?"

"Just some girl who works on the show."

"Why didn't you tell me that she was out with you as well? Why did you only mention Ashton and Paul?"

"Because I forgot."

"You forgot?" Marcia's tone was sarcastic.

"Why shouldn't I?" he asked impatiently. "She's a nobody to me. In fact, she just happened to be at the club. I don't know what Lonita and Andrea told you, but there was nothing going on between me and her."

"Did you dance with her?"

"She danced with all of us."

"Well, who did she go there with?"

"How should I know?"

Marcia was silent as she considered the information Jackson had given her. "Why would she be spending the whole night with you guys if she went there with somebody else?"

"I didn't ask her." His voice tightened with anger. "You know what, I don't care what your friends told you. I've told you the truth, and if it's not good enough for you, then there's nothing I can do."

Dissatisfied, Marcia stared at Jackson, willing him to say something—anything—that would make her feel better. All he had managed to do was confuse her even more. And the queasy feeling in her stomach was worsening.

"You know, Jackson," she finally said, "I don't know why you're getting so angry. If you're telling the truth—"

"I don't like being accused of lying."

Wearily, Marcia leaned against the headrest. "I wasn't accusing you, I was asking you. You're the one who started acting guilty."

"I resent being interrogated as if I've betrayed you. Where is your trust? You should know I wouldn't lie to you." He paused. "You know Lonita's never liked me."

Marcia was caught in a whirlwind of confusing emotions. She had never known Jackson to lie to her before. And she should trust him. But she had known Lonita almost all her life, and it was hard to believe that a dear friend and her sister would lie.

Marcia sighed. Her original instincts were probably right. Andrea and Lonita had misinterpreted what they had seen.

She turned to Jackson. "I'm sorry."

He took her hand in his. "I'm sorry too, okay?" Marcia nodded.

"I just don't want you thinking that I'm lying to you, because I'm not." Jackson leaned over and planted a kiss on Marcia's cheek. "And I'm definitely not cheating on you. I could never do that. I love you, Marcia."

She did not protest when he kissed her, but somewhere deep inside she sensed that she was a fool to believe him.

CHAPTER TWELVE

Gavin sat on his king-sized bed, a box of letters in his hand. Letters Marcia had written to him. He was missing her terribly, and he wanted to feel close to her again.

He'd called her all day Saturday, but nobody had been home and he didn't leave a message. Then he'd called her again on Sunday, and still he hadn't been able to reach her.

If his friends could see him now, they would certainly call him a lovesick puppy, reading letters from his former fiancée and reminiscing about how wonderful their relationship had once been. He was driving himself crazier than was necessary.

Choosing a lavender envelope, he pulled out the card. The front read, "Just because..." On the inside, "...I love you."

Marcia had written all kinds of wonderful things in the card, about how much he had changed her life, how much she loved him, how much she looked forward to their future together. Her writing was big and flowery and distinctly feminine.

He picked up another envelope, one with flowers printed on the outside. He withdrew the letter, written on matching stationery.

Dear Gavin,

I just can't believe how lucky I am. What did I ever do to deserve you?

Did you know there isn't one night that goes by when I don't dream about you? Big deal, right? To me it is. I've never felt this way in my life, and I must say, it's wonderful!

Do you feel the same way? I hope you do. I hope you don't think I'm crazy for writing this. It's just that you've changed my life for the better, and every day I am thankful for that.

I really hope I don't scare you off with this letter. Somehow, I don't think I will. I think you're as crazy about me as I am about you. I feel it every time I'm with you. Don't you?

Anyway, Gavin, I'm anxiously awaiting your call, and I can't wait to see you again.

Love,

Your soul mate, Marcia

Gavin smiled as memories of their extraordinary courtship flooded him. Everyone who saw them together commented that they were so much in love, a perfect couple. In every aspect, including physically, they seemed a perfect match.

Marcia was a true gem, beautiful both internally and externally. He remembered how she comforted him when he told her about Marcus, his young brother who had been killed by an overzealous police officer. Marcus's crime had been a mere traffic violation, and then he'd foolishly sped off when the officer tried to pull him over. The officer later made the excuse that Marcus "fit the description of a wanted suspect, one who was known to be armed and dangerous." He maintained he never planned to kill anyone—only to stop the car.

That was two years before Gavin started dating Marcia, but he still found it incredibly hard to deal with. He and Marcus had been as close as brothers could possibly be, and Marcus's death had crushed Gavin, not to mention the toll it took on his mother and younger sister. They were even more devastated when the police officer was cleared of any wrongdoing.

While nothing could ever bring his brother back, Marcia had certainly helped ease the pain. She had whispered words of comfort in his ear, held him as he expressed his feelings, and she had even cried with him. She never knew his brother, but she felt the pain along with him, and that was something Gavin could never forget.

He read several more letters, all written in the same spirit. Marcia professing her love for him. Marcia saying how much he had changed her life, how excited she was about their future.

Gavin returned the letters to the box. He couldn't take any more of this trip down memory lane. He needed a distraction.

He went downstairs to the kitchen and fixed himself a scotch on the rocks, a drink he resorted to only in times of extreme stress. This was the drink that had calmed his nerves several times after the breakup.

He winced as he took a sip, the strong liquor burning his throat as it went down.

The phone rang. He wasn't in the mood to talk to anyone, but he made his way to the living room phone and answered it before the machine picked up.

"Hello." He sounded harsh.

"Did I catch you at a bad time?"

His heartbeat accelerated as he heard the soft, sexy sound of Marcia's voice.

She said, "I know it's a bit late to call—"

"No, it's not." He took a deep breath. "This is a surprise."

"I need a friend, Gavin."

She sounded so weary, dispirited, that he wanted to fly to her and hold her in his arms.

"Talk," he said. "I'm a good listener."

"I was hoping that I could come over."

His heart leapt to his throat. He didn't know what was wrong, but he was willing to help her in whatever way he could, even if that meant just being her friend.

"You're welcome to come over any time you want," Gavin told her.

"How about now?"

Marcia drove down the dark street, sparse streetlights softly illuminating her path. She drove slowly, looking for the address Gavin had given her, wondering what on earth she was doing.

She could have talked to Lonita, or Andrea, or even her mother. But she had chosen Gavin. At nine o'clock at night, no less.

When she spotted his townhouse, she pulled into the driveway behind his Mustang and parked.

A lovely house, Marcia thought, observing the light-colored brick, the pink California-style roof, the large bay window. The kind of house they had talked about raising a family in.

Marcia hesitated. She was already confused enough. Coming here to see Gavin would only complicate matters.

But she could not make herself turn back. She rang the doorbell.

The door swung open, and Gavin greeted her with a heart-warming smile. "Come on in."

He ushered her in and took her jacket. She was wearing a pink cotton top that zipped up at the front, and a long black skirt. She folded her arms across her chest as she followed Gavin into the living room.

"I appreciate your letting me come over."

"My door is open to you any time, Marcia. I want you to know that."

"Thanks."

Marcia sat on a cream-colored leather sofa with a glass coffee table in front of it. The floor was polished oak, partially covered with a beautiful Persian rug. It was all neatly kept, but it didn't look lived in.

"I like it," she said, turning to Gavin.

Perched on the edge of a love seat, he looked remote and distant. Tonight of all nights she needed to be close to someone who cared about her.

She patted the spot next to her. "Won't you sit over here?"

Slowly, Gavin rose. To Marcia, it seemed as if he was being cautious, trying not to offend her, and she could certainly understand why.

When he sat next to her, she said, "I've had time to think about what you said, and you're right. It's a shame if we can't be friends. And that's why I am here. I need…a friend."

"I'm glad. I've missed having you in my life."

Marcia missed having him in her life as well, although until now, she hadn't wanted to admit it.

"So why did you need to see me?" His eyes conveyed a gentleness and softness that touched her soul.

"I—I'm not sure, to tell you the truth. There's just so much on my mind."

Gavin nodded. "Whenever you're ready, I'm ready. Do you want something to drink?"

She knew she should say no, but she found she was much tenser than she had expected. Maybe a glass of wine would help relax her.

"Do you have any wine?"

"Wine cooler. Lemon-lime."

"Fine."

Marcia watched Gavin walk to the kitchen. Her eyes traveled over his wide, brawny shoulders to his slim waist, then down to well-built thighs straining against the fabric of his cotton pants. He was still so beautiful. So incredibly sexy. The type of man any woman would be thrilled to have.

Jackson was sexy too, but his physical appeal meant nothing if he was lying to her.

Gavin returned. He poured some of the wine cooler into a glass, and when Marcia took the first cautious sip, she found the liquid delightfully refreshing. It tasted more like a fruit drink than anything alcoholic.

"I suppose I should just come right out and tell you what's going on, if I can figure out what I'm really thinking," Marcia said.

"Sure."

"I…I don't know what will happen between Jackson and me. Things aren't going the way I hoped they would."

Gavin raised an eyebrow. "What's the problem?"

"Until yesterday, I didn't think there was a problem," Marcia explained. "We had our little spats—every couple does. And I noticed that Jackson had started drinking too much. But that was something I could deal with."

Marcia took another sip of her drink. "Yesterday, Lonita and Andrea told me that they saw Jackson out at a club on Friday night. And he was with another woman."

"There may be an explanation for that," Gavin said cautiously.

"That's what I thought at first. I mean, I knew they wouldn't lie to me, but I figured they were mistaken. Misinterpreted what they saw."

"But you don't think that anymore?"

Marcia twirled the stem of the wineglass between her fingers. "I think Jackson is lying to me."

"Why?"

"Because..." She broke off and stood, suddenly unable to go on. Despite her efforts to stay strong, a soft sob escaped her.

Gavin rose to his feet beside her and took her in his arms. "Don't cry, Marcia. I hate to see you cry."

She pulled away, out of the shelter of his arms, away from his protective warmth...and immediately felt cold and alone.

She stammered, "I—I have to go. I never should have come here. I don't know why I did." She looked up at Gavin and saw concern in his eyes. Her resolve weakened. She added softly, "Maybe because I can't stop thinking about you."

"You've been thinking about me?"

She hesitated. "The way it used to be. I...can't seem to stop."

Gavin took a deep breath. "What are you saying?"

"Nothing. I don't know. I'm confused, Gavin. And I have to go now." But despite her words, she did not move.

Gavin reached out and touched Marcia's mouth with his thumb, feathering it along the entire surface of her full lips.

Her mouth parted slightly, and then, as unexpectedly to her as it must have been to Gavin, they were in each other's arms. The feel of him, the musky scent of his cologne, the taste of his mouth, were so familiar, so right, so welcome after four years.

Marcia ran her fingers up Gavin's back, exploring his taut muscles, enjoying how it felt to hold him again. It had been so long. Slipping her hands around his neck, she found the soft, curly strands at the nape and played with them.

Gavin splayed his hands across her back, pulling her close. Her breasts pressed against his chest, and she moaned into his mouth. She needed this, needed to be with someone who cared about her, someone she cared about. Holding him tighter, she deepened the kiss.

Murmuring her name, Gavin ran his hands down her back and over her buttocks, pulling her against his arousal.

Suddenly, Marcia tore her lips from his. What on earth was she doing?

Still holding her tight, Gavin rained kisses along her cheek and jawbone.

Marcia put a hand on his chest. "Don't."

Immediately, Gavin stopped. Loosening his hold he looked down at her his expression a mixture of desire and confusion.

"Gavin, I'm sorry. I can't do this. Jackson may be…but I can't. This is wrong."

"No, I am sorry, Marcia. You came here to talk, and I—" He grimaced ruefully. "Forgive me."

Gavin could have been angry but instead accepted the blame. Stroking his face, Marcia smiled at him.

"There's no need to apologize, Gavin. Thank you. I mean, for being here when I needed a friend."

"My door is always open."

"I should go now." Marcia picked up her purse. One part of her didn't want to leave, but the other part knew she should.

When she was at the door, Gavin said, "You're still as beautiful as you used to be. I hope you know that."

His words made her heart accelerate. Despite the years and their problems, she was still attracted to him. That was a truth she could no longer deny.

Softly, she said, "Perhaps I'll call you tomorrow."

CHAPTER THIRTEEN

Jackson wasn't due home until late evening, and Marcia was glad. She was too confused to deal with him or anyone else.

Tearing off a piece of grilled cheese sandwich she had prepared, Marcia nibbled on it but found it tasteless. She dropped the sandwich on the plate and rose from the kitchen table, sauntering to the floor-to-ceiling windows in the solarium.

Leaning her forehead against the cool glass, she looked out. Leaves had turned a variety of vibrant colors and many had fallen from the trees. But the picturesque early fall day was the last thing on Marcia's mind.

What was on her mind was what happened last night. Why did she go over to Gavin's? This question and others had plagued her ever since she awoke in the morning. The memory of her trip to his home seemed like a dream, it was so bizarre. So unexpected. But so extraordinary.

When he took her in his arms, it was as if no time had passed since the last time they embraced. How had she gotten so caught up in her past feelings? Why, after everything, had she succumbed to his kiss with such abandon? And why, deep in her heart, did she not regret it?

Because she still had feelings for him.

But how deep were those feelings? Was she merely trying to resolve her earlier feelings for him by getting close to him last night? After all, their relationship had ended so abruptly before, and Marcia had never truly gotten over it.

And, if she still had feelings for Gavin, where did that leave Jackson?

Marcia gritted her teeth as she thought of Jackson in the arms of another woman, in another woman's bed. She didn't have any proof that he had fooled around on her, but she had gut instinct. For quite a while, she had sensed that something was wrong with their relationship, and maybe this was it.

Frowning, Marcia went into the living room and huddled on the love seat. Her feelings were too jumbled. Even if Jackson was seeing someone else, she didn't want to run back into Gavin's arms on the rebound. That wouldn't be fair to her or to Gavin. But what if her feelings for Gavin were stronger than she cared to admit?

Her brain felt as if it might explode. Jumping off the love seat, she headed for the door. She needed to get out.

She needed to clear her mind.

Two hours later, Marcia was at her parents' doorstep. She had simply gotten into her car and started to drive, and this was where she ended up.

Her mother's face lit up when she saw her at the door. "My baby! I'm so glad to see you."

Marcia hugged her mother. "I'm glad to see you, too."

Mrs. Robertson released her daughter. "What brings you by?"

"I just needed to see you. I needed my mother." Hearing footsteps, Marcia looked up to see her brother racing down the stairs. "Dwayne! What's up?"

"Nothing much." Reluctantly, the teenager submitted to her hug. "I've got a lot of homework to do."

"That's a part of life."

"I don't know why I bother. My homeroom teacher hates me."

"What's your homeroom?"

"History. With Mr. Young. He's a pain in the—" His mother's warning glance stopped him from completing his sentence.

He walked into the living room, his shoulders drooping.

Marcia followed him. "So why does your homeroom teacher hate you?"

"Because he's racist."

Marcia gave Dwayne a skeptical look. "You say that every year."

"You don't have to believe me, but I'm the one who has to put up with it, and I know Mr. Young is racist. He doesn't respect my view of history. All he wants me to talk about is white people, what they've done. He doesn't even think blacks have done anything worthwhile."

Marcia couldn't argue with that. It was frustrating how little was taught about black culture and history in the schools. And the minuscule fragments black children did hear were all negative. Rarely were students taught about the blacks who contributed to society and made a positive difference.

"Maybe that's something you should start a petition about." When her brother eyed her cynically, Marcia said, "I'm serious. Get all the other minorities at the school to sign a petition saying they want to have their history represented in the curriculum. There are a lot of Asians, East Indians, and other minority groups who probably feel the same way. Then take that petition to the principal."

"I never thought about that."

Marcia rubbed his arm affectionately. "I have a ton of books on black history that I can lend you. You can even suggest these books to your principal."

She left him to ponder the idea. Her brother was a wonderful kid, and very intelligent. If he was rebellious and unmotivated to cooperate in school, a course of positive action might turn him around. Dwayne's real problem was that he felt alienated from the school system.

Her mother was upstairs bent over the ironing board. Marcia dropped onto the bed.

"Where's Dad?"

"Still at the shop. He won't be home until after seven."

Marcia watched her mother silently for a few minutes, then decided to come right out and speak about what was bothering her.

"Mom, did you ever have any problems with Dad? I mean serious problems? The kind you break up over?"

Mrs. Robertson looked at her daughter quizzically "We all have problems. No relationship is easy."

"Yeah, but did Dad ever do anything you considered unforgivable?"

"I guess if he did, I wouldn't be with him now. What's this about, Marcia?"

Marcia shrugged.

"What has Jackson done?"

"Nothing, really. At least nothing that I know for certain."

Mrs. Robertson rested the iron on the ironing board and gave her full attention to her daughter. "The last time I saw you, you were upset about something. I could tell. Is it his work?"

"No. His work couldn't be going better."

"But he has less time to spend with you."

"That's not the problem."

"Then what is?"

Marcia got off the bed and started pacing. "The problem is that I don't know if he wants to be in this relationship anymore. I've been told that he's fooling around, and...I just don't know what to do."

"Do you know for sure that he's fooling around?"

"No. I asked him, but he denied it—of course."

"And you don't believe him?"

"It's more like a gut instinct. If he's not fooling around, then something else is wrong."

"And what did you want to talk to me about?" Mrs. Robertson asked matter-of-factly. "Do you want me to tell you whether or not I think you should leave him?"

"I'm not sure I want to leave him."

"Then what are you really asking?"

Marcia faced her mother. "I guess I'm asking you to tell me how you know when it's worth it to fight for a relationship."

"That all depends on whether or not you love him."

"And whether or not he loves me."

Mrs. Robertson approached Marcia and gently cupped her chin. "Is that the problem? You don't think he loves you?"

Marcia shrugged. "I don't know, Mom. If he's fooling around, then how can he love me? And if he doesn't love me, then why am I wasting my time? Did you ever feel this way about Dad?"

Mrs. Robertson shook her head. "With your father, I always knew he loved me, but there were other things we needed to work on."

"Like what?"

"Like open communication. Letting each other know when we were hurt, that kind of stuff. We both had a problem not expressing our feelings—especially our anger. And that just made everything worse."

Marcia looked at her mother with increased interest. "So what did you do?"

"I finally sat your father down one day and had a long talk with him. Since then, we've both made an effort to be open and honest."

"It must have worked, since you're still together."

"You have to keep working at it. It doesn't work itself." Mrs. Robertson placed a reassuring arm around her daughter's shoulder. "My advice to you is to be open and honest about your feelings with Jackson. If he cares about you, he'll want to listen. And if you love each other, you'll work it out."

Marcia hugged her mother. "Thanks, Mom."

As soon as Marcia opened the door to her condo, she remembered that she had forgotten to go to the store and pick up some bread. The fridge was almost bare, containing only milk, butter, and some jam. With Jackson's steady acting job, he ate on the set every day and never came home hungry. Because of that, she tended to buy groceries only when the need arose.

She didn't mind the ten-minute walk to the corner store. The crisp night air was good for body and spirit.

She bought eggs and vanilla ice cream, as well as bread. The ice cream would soften on the way home, but she didn't mind. She liked her ice cream soft.

Again, the night air felt blissful on her face, gently soothing her and ridding her mind of stress. As she neared the condominium, she wished the walk could have been longer. She would have continued her peaceful stroll if it weren't for the ice cream.

She noticed a black sports car parked at the front of the building but didn't give it much attention, except to note that it was a really nice car. As she got closer, she could see the dark shapes of a couple locked in a passionate embrace. Maybe they believed themselves sheltered from curious eyes, but they had not taken the streetlight into account.

As she passed the car, she noticed that the woman was a blonde. And that the man whom the woman was kissing was Jackson.

She stopped, her stomach twisting into a tight knot. Perhaps the streetlight and her own uneasiness were playing a trick on her. She closed her eyes, then slowly opened them.

There was no doubt. It was Jackson with another woman.

Bastard! Marcia wanted to yell, but her voice would not obey. And then the tears came. Tears of humiliation and rage. How could he do this to her? And right in front of their building, no less! Even if she hadn't seen him, someone else who knew them surely might have.

Marcia didn't know where she got the strength, but somehow she made it to the front door of her building. Too upset to wait for the elevator, she took the stairs to the tenth floor, running every step of the way.

She slammed the apartment door behind her, dropping the groceries to the floor. She didn't care about the ice cream anymore. She didn't care about the bread or the eggs. She was aware only of the deep hurt inside her. Even with her earlier suspicions, actually seeing Jackson kissing someone else came as a horrible blow.

Her relationship was over. She didn't want to be with Jackson one more second, let alone one more night. But this was his place, and as much as she wanted to, she couldn't kick him out.

She would have to leave. Wiping at her tears, she stormed into the bedroom and grabbed a suitcase from the closet. She opened drawers and began throwing everything she owned into the suitcase.

"Marcia."

She hadn't heard Jackson enter the apartment or the bedroom. Startled, she whirled. In the span of a heartbeat, she raised her hand and slapped him.

Clutching the grocery bag she had dropped, Jackson stared openmouthed.

Her breath came in labored gasps. "How dare you do this to me? How dare you!"

"What are you talking about?" He pointed to the open drawers and suitcase. "And what the hell is going on here?"

"As if you don't know," she said bitterly. "You—forget it! I'm not wasting another breath on you!"

Marcia saw the flicker of understanding in his eyes. He knew what she was talking about.

He began slowly, "Let me explain. Whatever it is you think you saw—"

"Think?" She could scarcely speak for anger. "Don't go there, Jackson. You know what I saw! God, I've been such a fool!"

"That girl—she just gave me a ride home."

"I'll bet she gave you a ride."

"It's not like that. She's just a friend."

Friend...The simple word silenced her and caused feelings of confusion to infiltrate her anger. She had asked Gavin to be her friend. And last night, she had kissed him. Jackson had kissed another woman. Were his actions worse than her own?

They had to be. She had turned to Gavin after things had gone bad in her relationship. Who knew how long Jackson had been having an affair or how many different women he'd been seeing? Still, she felt guilt over her own actions, guilt over the fact that she had been as weak as Jackson, and that guilt fueled her anger.

"Just tell me this, Jackson! Is she the same woman from the Film Festival party? Or the one you took dancing? Or is she someone else altogether?"

"Give me a minute to explain—"

"Spare me." Marcia zipped up the suitcase and pulled it off the bed. She hadn't even come close to getting all her belongings, but she couldn't stand to be in the same room with Jackson for one more minute. "I'll return your key after I've had a chance to get all my things. I'll make sure to do that when you're working."

She marched past him through the bedroom door, and he didn't try to stop her. But when she reached the apartment door, she heard him plead, "Please, Marcia. Don't go."

The humble note in his voice brought fresh tears to her eyes. But why should she cry? He didn't deserve her tears.

And then she bolted through the door, not daring to look back.

CHAPTER FOURTEEN

After driving to both Andrea's and Lonita's and finding nobody home, Marcia was crying so hard that her entire body was shaking. Her parents' place was a half-hour drive across the city, but with her hands trembling she knew she could not make it there.

She pulled onto a side street and parked. What was she going to do? She felt like crawling into a hole until the pain subsided. She wasn't cut out for relationships. She'd had two serious ones in her life, and they had both failed. First, Gavin had broken her heart; now Jackson. How much heartache could one person endure?

The sound of squealing tires interrupted Marcia's thoughts and reminded her that she couldn't stay on the street all night. Her mind drifted to Gavin. He had offered to be a friend, and he lived nearby.

Marcia started the car and began to drive. She hoped he was home.

"Good Lord, Marcia!" Gavin exclaimed when he opened his front door. Her eyes were red and swollen. Mascara stained her cheeks. "What happened?"

She fell into his arms and burst into tears. "Oh, Gavin!"

His heart ached to see her in such pain. He wanted to know what had happened, who had hurt her like this, but he did not ask. He merely held her as she cried.

"It's over," she sobbed, as if in answer to his unspoken question. "Gavin, just hold me."

He ran his hand over her shoulder-length black hair, trying to soothe her. As she clung to him, her body shaking as she cried, he realized how fragile and vulnerable she was. He wished he could do something more to help her.

"What happened?" he asked softly.

"It's true. Everything...Andrea and Lonita were right!"

"About Jackson?"

"Y-Yes. I left him, Gavin. It's over."

Angry, Gavin clenched his teeth. How could Jackson do this to her? Did he even care about her? Had he ever? And how did she find out?

"Marcia, are you sure?"

Inhaling short, erratic breaths, she slipped out of his embrace. She wiped her eyes and smoothed her hair. "You know what they say. Seeing is believing."

"You saw him with her?"

Marcia nodded. "Right in front of our building...in a car. I had gone to the store and was walking by, and that's when I saw them."

Gavin groaned. "I'm so sorry, Marcia."

"It's like a bad nightmare. I never thought—"

"Because you trusted him."

A bitter expression clouded her face. "He said he loved me, but it was all a lie."

"Marcia, some men are like that. They have a good woman, but that's not enough. Now that Jackson is a celebrity, he's bound to have women coming on to him. Maybe he just got weak."

Marcia flashed Gavin an indignant look. "Weak? So because he's a star now, he can do this kind of thing, and I'm not supposed to get upset?"

"That's not what I'm saying."

"I know." She placed a hand over her forehead. "I'm sorry. I'm just mad. I did see him with that woman at a Film Festival party. But just because he's well-known now doesn't give him the right to do what he did."

"Of course not. Maybe he's just—"

"I don't care," Marcia cut in. "He's got a lot of nerve. He always talked about being so strong, about not getting caught up in the business and all its ills. Then, he started drinking too much. Now this."

Gavin didn't know what to do or say. Nothing would make her feel better, except time.

"You can stay here tonight, if you want," he offered.

She looked up at him with glistening eyes. "Thanks. Tomorrow, I'll call Lonita and ask if I can stay with her until I can find a place of my own."

"Why don't we go into the living room and sit? The doorway isn't quite as comfortable as a sofa."

She smiled a little, as he hoped she would.

"Can I get you anything?" he asked as they walked to the living room. "Water? Tea?"

"Tea would be nice." Marcia sat on the sofa.

It took Gavin a few minutes to prepare her a hot cup of mint tea. Gratefully, she took it, eagerly taking a sip.

"You remembered." She smiled at him. "My favorite tea."

Her smile warmed him all over. "I'm happy to please. Do you need…a T-shirt? Something to sleep in?"

"I've got a suitcase with some of my things in the car. I will need a toothbrush, though. I forgot that."

"I've got an extra one. Let me get your suitcase."

Marcia handed him the keys to her car, showing him which one opened the door. Gavin couldn't help thinking how soft her skin was, how smooth to the touch.

When he went out to her car, he stopped for a moment, letting the cool air clear his thoughts. He was ecstatic that Marcia had turned to him after she left Jackson. He couldn't help but hope…

But it wouldn't do to get carried away. She had just ended a relationship and needed time and space to sort out her feelings. She considered him a friend, someone she could trust.

He remembered the other night, when they had kissed. But those memories were dangerous. Inflammatory. Banishing them to the back of his mind, he grabbed her suitcase and carried it to his bedroom.

Marcia followed him. "Where can I sleep?"

"Right here. You take the bed."

"But where will you sleep?"

"On the sofa."

Marcia's eyes locked with his, her expression unreadable. Gavin was the one to finally turn away.

"Let me just get what I need." He rummaged through a drawer and took out a pair of pajama pants. Turning back to Marcia, he said, "It's all yours."

He walked past her quickly. She was too tempting, even with her hair disheveled and her makeup messy from crying. She was just too damn beautiful, no matter what the occasion.

Gavin took a comforter out of the linen closet and turned to find Marcia behind him. He cursed silently under his breath, frustrated at the sudden heat sensation that flooded his loins. "You scared me."

"Sorry," she said. "Can I have a towel?"

Gavin fought to control the urge to take her in his arms. He reached into the closet and withdrew a towel. "Here you go."

"Thanks, Gavin." She touched his face gently, briefly. Heart pounding, he watched as she retreated to the bedroom. She was so incredibly beautiful. And he loved her.

Just before she closed the door, she turned and said in a voice as smooth as satin, "Sweet dreams."

And his dreams were sweet indeed.

In his dreams, he held Marcia in his arms all night, enjoying the feel of her, the scent of her, just being with her. They were together, the way he knew they were meant to be.

In the morning, he entered his bedroom quietly and saw her fast asleep, lying on her stomach. One shapely leg was exposed beneath the blanket. It took all the willpower he possessed to stay away from her when his hands ached to stroke the length of smooth golden skin.

But he would not violate the trust she had placed in him. For now, it was enough to know that she no longer lived with Jackson.

Gavin searched the closet for suitable work clothes, then slipped out of the bedroom. Marcia hadn't even stirred, which was good. She needed to rest.

He dressed in the bathroom. When he looked in the mirror, the reflection he saw staring back at him had a sparkle in his eyes.

That man had something to hope for.

CHAPTER FIFTEEN

Marcia turned in bed, stretched, then opened her eyes. As she inspected the unfamiliar surroundings, she was suddenly confused. Where was she?

Then she remembered. She was at Gavin's place. In his bed.

The townhouse was extraordinarily quiet. Marcia threw off the covers and sauntered downstairs to the living room. Gavin wasn't there. There was also no sign that he had even slept on the sofa. He must have folded the comforter and put it away.

That was just like the Gavin she remembered—extraordinarily neat. He had always said that he couldn't relax in a messy environment.

Marcia looked at the clock. It was after eleven a.m. She hadn't realized she'd slept so long without once waking up to stew over Jackson's rotten behavior. Without even having a nightmare about the baby. Maybe this was a sign that she had done the right thing by leaving Jackson.

Marcia opened a window and inhaled the cool, fresh morning air. She would have to call her agent soon, but first she must call Lonita and make arrangements to stay with her. Unlike her sister, Lonita would understand that she needed space.

She must also check her pager, which was in her purse in the bedroom. She went back upstairs. There were no pages from her agent or from her sister and friend, but at least two from Jackson. His latest call had been four hours ago.

Marcia scowled. He'd have a long wait if he thought that she would phone. She had nothing to say to him.

Sitting on the bed, she ran her hand over the sheets. Gavin's familiar scent lingered there, and to her surprise, that gave her some measure of comfort. She didn't feel alone. And she was happy that she and Gavin could be friends, especially now.

Picking up the phone, she dialed the daycare number where Lonita worked.

It took a while, but finally Lonita came to the phone. "Hey, girlfriend. You hardly call me at work. Everything okay?"

"As a matter of fact, no. Things are bad. That's why I'm calling. I need a place to stay."

"You left Jackson."

"Yes. But I'll tell you about it later. I just need to know if I can stay with you. Until I find a place of my own."

"Of course you can. Where are you now?"

"I'll tell you that later, too. What time will you be home?"

"About six-thirty. But if you want, you can come here and get the key."

Marcia wouldn't leave Gavin's house before he returned home. "Six-thirty is fine. I'll see you then."

Marcia called her agent and gave him the phone number where he could reach her. She was thankful that the acting job she had landed wouldn't be shooting until next week. That gave her several days to pull herself together and to remove her belongings from Jackson's place.

It would be a long wait until Gavin came home, but Marcia didn't feel like leaving the house. All she wanted to do today was relax. She showered, then dressed in black slacks and a gray knit top.

Venturing to the kitchen, she inventoried the refrigerator. Milk, jam, juice, and bread. From what Marcia remembered, Gavin wasn't a very good cook. He probably ate take-out all the time.

That's what she could do to thank him, she realized. Make him a nice dinner. After eating some toast, she hopped into her black Toyota Camry and drove around the neighborhood to locate the nearest grocery store. She bought white kidney beans, soya sauce, parboiled rice, several vegetables, and two packages of oxtail.

Back at Gavin's place, she prepared West Indian-style oxtail and a tossed salad. While the rice simmered, she started to tidy up the bedroom. As she bent over her suitcase at the foot of Gavin's bed, her toe hit something hard behind the dark bedspread ruffle. Darn, that hurt! What surprised her, though, was that the very tidy Gavin would store stuff under his bed, the catchall hiding place for the not-so-tidy.

On hands and knees, she lifted the bedspread and peered under the bed. The culprit was a metal barbell. She pushed it farther back and noticed another item. A shoebox.

She returned to her packing, but somehow the shoebox stayed on her mind. Gavin would never store shoes under his bed. Neither would he clutter up his environment with an empty box. Not the Gavin she knew.

Finally, curiosity getting the better of her, Marcia snatched the mysteriously tempting box from under the bed. Sitting cross-legged on the floor, she whipped off the cover.

The first thing she saw was a red envelope with the name "Gavin" written in her handwriting. Quickly, she flipped through the contents of the box and realized that it contained probably all the letters and cards she had sent him.

Her hand hovered over the letters. She shouldn't be snooping.

But these were cards and letters *she* had given him, so it wouldn't do any harm to re-read them.

She could not resist. She opened the first envelope—and it made no sense that she should feel guilty doing it. This was a Valentine's Day card she had given him.

Will you be my Valentine? Not just today, but every day. I love you so much.

Marcia.

The memory of their time together hit her like a ton of bricks. That was the Valentine's Day she had bought a sexy red lace bra and matching panties and modeled them for him. Gavin had shown his appreciation all night long, feasting on her body and giving her extreme pleasure.

That was also the last Valentine's Day they had shared as a couple.

Marcia replaced the card and moved on to the next item, a letter she had written in the first year of their courtship.

Dear Gavin,

I miss you already! You may think that is impossible since we were just together. But I do. Maybe it's because I know you will be gone tomorrow. That's a whole day, and I'm not sure

I can stand not seeing you! Of course, I look forward to seeing you when you come back. I treasure every moment we share, and I wish I could have you twenty-four/seven. I just love you so much.

Marcia.

Her throat constricted as she remembered the three wonderful years she had spent loving Gavin. How could a love like that end as bitterly as it did? She wiped at a stray tear, then moved on to the next letter. And the next.

In all the letters and cards she had written to him, she had professed her undying love. Tucked among the letters were photos of her and of them together, and pieces of paper on which Gavin had doodled their names in a heart, or had simply written, "I love Marcia."

Now she felt even guiltier than when she first opened the box. She hadn't kept his letters and cards but had burned every one of them. She hadn't had the heart to burn the photos of them, but she had stashed them away in her parents' basement.

She wiped at another tear rolling down her cheek as she gazed at one particular photo. How well she remembered the day it was taken…during a trip to Niagara Falls, where Gavin had surprised her by proposing.

In the picture, taken by a helpful stranger, they posed at the railing of the falls. Gavin's arms were wrapped tightly around her, and she was holding her left hand high so that her pear-shaped diamond was in plain view.

They had spent a glorious, wonderfully romantic two days together, dining, seeing the sights, making love in their heart-shaped Jacuzzi. Her life with Gavin had been nothing short of perfect. And her life without him had been nothing short of hell.

Then she met Jackson two years after the breakup. She had just returned from Vancouver, the place where she had lived out her worst nightmare, and was starting to put her life back together.

The last thing she wanted was a new relationship. But Jackson was sweet and persistent, and she liked him very much. He was a welcome distraction from the dark, painful memories of the past. A past she never shared with Jackson. She couldn't. She wanted her secrets to remain dead and buried.

Marcia thrust the box back under the bed. She wished that her memories of those happier days with Gavin had remained dead and buried, too.

"Something smells very good."

Gavin's voice in the hallway startled her. Scrambling to her feet, Marcia positioned herself over her suitcase just before he entered the bedroom.

"Hi," he said, his smile warming her heart.

"Hi." She hoped her guilt didn't show on her face. But Gavin didn't seem suspicious. Turning back to the bed, she folded her clothes and placed them in the suitcase.

Gavin joined her. "Did you get to talk to Lonita about staying with her?"

"Yes. It's all arranged. Thanks for letting me stay here last night."

"No problem."

Her heart was beating faster because of his close proximity. Would he try to kiss her? Would she let him?

Gavin asked, "Is that oxtail you're making?"

Marcia felt slightly disappointed that he didn't try to kiss her. What was wrong with her? Why was she getting caught up in the past? Going through all those letters and photos had affected her more than she realized. The sooner she got out of here, away from Gavin, the better.

She zipped up her suitcase. "Yes, I made you some dinner. It was the least I could do."

"You're not leaving yet, are you? You will share dinner with me?"

She should leave immediately. Her heart was sending her brain mixed signals, and she was too vulnerable at the moment. But she said, "All right. I'll just check on the rice."

Gavin placed a warm hand on her arm. "Let me."

"And how would you know when rice is cooked?"

"Rice is something I learned to cook in Japan. Finish up in here, and I'll get dinner ready."

He disappeared, leaving Marcia feeling flustered. Even though she knew he wanted to get back together, he wasn't pressuring her. He was being considerate of her feelings. And she felt more drawn to him than ever.

She grabbed her suitcase and took it to the car. When she returned, Gavin announced that dinner was served.

He seated her at the dining table. "I poured you sparkling white grape juice instead of wine, since you'll be driving."

"Thank you." He was being so sensitive it was hard not to be drawn to him. He really was a wonderful man.

As they ate, Marcia noticed that Gavin devoured his food. It had probably been a long time since his last home-cooked meal. That made her think of his mother. "How is your mother doing?"

His eyes turned as dark as sable, and Marcia realized immediately that something was wrong.

"I guess you don't know that she had cancer."

Marcia gasped. "Cancer? How awful."

Gavin nodded grimly. "Breast cancer. But she was lucky. They caught it in time. They were able to operate and remove the tumor before it had spread anywhere else."

"Oh, thank God," Marcia said, relieved. She admired Cicely Williams, who had embraced her with open arms. She felt badly that she hadn't called her after the breakup with Gavin. "Did she have to lose her breast?"

Gavin shook his head. "No. They cut out the tumor, and she had several radiation and chemotherapy treatments. She's been in remission now for three months."

"Three months! So this was recent."

"That's the reason I came home. From Japan."

"Well, that's understandable." She hesitated. "Actually, when Lonita told me that you spent three years teaching in Japan, I was surprised. You always said you wanted to be close to your family."

"You mean it's what I said when you wanted me to move to Vancouver with you." Gavin's gaze met and held hers. "After you left, I just wasn't the same. I was depressed, irritable, withdrawn. At times, I didn't know how I would make it through the day."

Marcia's back stiffened. "Are you trying to make me feel guilty?"

"No. I'm trying to explain. I was a fool to give you that blasted ultimatum—to make you choose. And when you left, I felt like I had died inside."

"I know the feeling," she said softly. "So that's why you went overseas?"

"My mother encouraged me to go. I didn't really want to leave her, not after what happened to Marcus. But she insisted that the teaching experience might help me find a permanent job here. And she said I needed to get away from Toronto if I was ever going to get over you."

Marcia remembered her own pain and wondered if Gavin's had been as intense.

He chuckled mirthlessly. "The funny thing is, I never did get over you. It didn't matter that I went halfway around the world, you were still in my heart."

Marcia tensed involuntarily, and Gavin saw her reaction.

"I'm not trying to pressure you, Marcia. I'm just telling you the truth. That's how I felt. When my mother got sick, I quit teaching over there and rushed home. I'd lost my brother, and when I feared I might lose my mother, I realized how short life really is."

He reached out and took Marcia's hand. "And that's when I knew that, if it's the last thing I do, I will try to get you back in my life."

"It wasn't easy for me," Marcia said defensively. "I hope you realize that. Leaving you and the love we shared was the hardest thing I ever had to do."

The hardest, next to accepting that her baby was stillborn. But that Gavin would never know. He couldn't.

Gavin squeezed her hand. "I think we needed this talk. When we split, that was it. We weren't friends, and we didn't stay in touch. We never discussed how we felt."

"It was too hard," Marcia replied softly.

"I know."

Her insides were churning. It hurt her more than she had anticipated to talk about the past with the man who had caused her all that grief. But it had been helpful to learn that he had suffered too, that it hadn't been easy to say goodbye to their love.

She rose. "Thank you for everything. I'll be in touch."

Gavin rose as well. "Maybe we can get together tomorrow?"

"Why don't I call you tomorrow and let you know?"

"Okay."

She made her way to the door, and Gavin followed. She needed to put some time and distance between them. Remembering the baby had her feeling depressed…and guilty. Gavin should know he had lost a child, but she could never tell him. He would hate her if he knew.

"Is everything okay, Marcia?"

"Yes," she lied.

"You don't seem okay. But I think I know what's bothering you."

Marcia grew rigid. He couldn't know. There was no way…

"Most of your things are still at Jackson's, aren't they? And it'll be hard going back there to get all your stuff."

"You're right," she said, knowing full well that wasn't what bothered her.

"I can help you move out when you're ready."

"Thanks for the offer. I'll let you know if I need your help."

He nodded, then planted a soft kiss on her forehead before she could back away. "Take care, Marcia."

CHAPTER SIXTEEN

"It's over." Marcia spoke with a calmness that surprised her, considering she felt sick to her stomach every time she thought about what Jackson had done to her.

She sat on Lonita's sofa with her knees drawn to her chest, her head resting against one knee. Andrea sat to her right; Lonita to her left. After leaving Gavin's, she had called her sister and asked her to meet her at Lonita's because she had something to tell her.

"It's over?" Andrea wrinkled her brow. "So does that mean…?"

"I moved out," Marcia said. "You two were right. Jackson has been cheating on me, and that's not something I can live with."

"What happened?" asked Lonita. "Because you didn't believe us when we first told you."

"And I'm sorry I didn't." Swinging her legs off the sofa, Marcia paused. "But there was no room for doubt when I saw them with my own eyes."

"You didn't!" Andrea exclaimed.

Marcia nodded tersely. "Unfortunately. Well, I guess it's fortunate because now I know the truth. Do you believe he had the nerve to be parked in front of our condo, getting busy right there in her car?"

Lonita's mouth dropped open. "For real?"

"It's bad enough to learn the truth, but to see it—" Marcia inhaled deeply, trying to control her troubled emotions. Showing weakness was something she didn't like doing.

Andrea patted her sister's hand. "This is such a shame. You two have been together so long."

"But obviously our relationship didn't mean a thing to him."

Lonita slid closer. "I'm so sorry." She hugged Marcia. "Before all this, I really thought he was the one."

Not wanting to get emotional, Marcia shrugged. Even though she had accepted the reality of Jackson's unfaithfulness, it was hard to think about the bitter betrayal. It was hard to think about how little regard Jackson had for her feelings.

"Jackson is a fool," Andrea said. "One of these days, he's gonna look at his life, and he won't be very happy. Then he's gonna to say, 'Damn! Marcia was the best thing that ever happened to me.' And by then, you'll be happily married with five kids."

"And you know his moment in the sun will have passed. We'll probably see him working at Burger King. 'Would you like fries with that?'" Lonita laughed at her joke, and so did Andrea. And despite Marcia's inner turmoil, she chuckled.

"Does any of this really surprise us anymore?" Lonita asked rhetorically. "Look at me and Thomas. I thought we would get married, until I found out he was already married. The bottom line here is that all men are dogs. Am I right?"

"You know it," Andrea agreed heartily.

"How can men say they love you, then hurt you like this?" Marcia asked.

"Some men love you, even though they're dogs," was Lonita's matter-of-fact reply.

Marcia shook her head. "I don't think that's possible. If you love someone, sure you can make a mistake—but not all the time."

"Men will be that way 'cause women put up with it," Lonita said, a knowing expression on her face.

Andrea opened her mouth to speak, but Marcia quickly cut her off. "You better not disagree with that one, given your track record with Curtis."

"Have you told your mother?" Lonita asked.

"I called her this afternoon."

"Mom always liked Jackson," Andrea said. "How did she take the news?"

"She said it was better that I found out now, as opposed to later."

"Men!" Andrea heaved an agitated sigh. "Why can't we just live without them?"

Lonita raised a suggestive brow. "We all know the answer to that."

While Andrea and Lonita laughed, Marcia's mind drifted to Gavin. He'd been completely different from Jackson. That, in part, had been what had attracted her to Jackson; she had wanted no reminders of her passionate lost love.

Unlike Jackson, Gavin had never cheated on Marcia. To this day she would swear to that, despite everything. In a way, it would have been so much easier if he *had* cheated on her. If there had been a tangible explanation for their sudden parting.

Lonita rose, stretching like a cat. "Why don't we order some Chinese food, rent a movie, and forget about men tonight?"

"Great idea," said Andrea.

Marcia slapped her thigh. "Sounds perfect."

The evening was filled with lots of laughter, which was exactly what Marcia needed. For a few hours she was able to forget about Jackson, about Gavin and the baby, and her mixed emotions.

But as she lay awake in bed that night, she found herself missing Gavin. His warm smile, his thoughtfulness. There was something about him now, so like the Gavin she had first met and fallen in love with. But those thoughts were hazardous to her heart.

He wanted to reconcile. After everything, could she take that risk? Why was she even considering it? Maybe she was indeed losing her mind.

Four-and-a-half years ago…

Marcia kissed Gavin deeply. She murmured, "Oh, I hope I got that part. I think I did a really good read."

He smiled despite the fact that he was feeling more and more uneasy with her decision to be an actress. She had been getting more prominent auditions, and it shouldn't have surprised him that sooner or later she would have to do a romantic scene.

"You're not going to kiss some other guy like that, are you?" Gavin asked. The way he posed the question made it obvious what he thought her answer should be.

"Sweetheart," Marcia kissed him again. "Of course not. I mean, sure, I'll have to make the kiss look realistic, but I won't feel anything. In fact, I've heard from other people that kissing scenes and love scenes are the worst to do. They're completely uncomfortable."

That didn't make Gavin feel any better. Kissing was kissing, and he certainly didn't want another man kissing the woman he loved. If only she would get a stable job, something sensible and satisfying—like teaching was for him.

"I don't know how you handle that crazy business. Have you ever thought of getting out of it?"

Marcia laughed and ran her fingers along his cheek. "Not a chance. I love everything about acting—making words on paper come alive, the insight it gives people into their own lives—I wouldn't trade it for anything."

"Not even me?"

Gavin drifted in and out of sleep, in and out of dreams. His king-sized bed felt very large. And very empty. Rolling onto his back, he linked his fingers behind his head and stared at the ceiling. If only he hadn't forced Marcia to choose between him and her career back then. What a jerk he was!

He had been calling himself a jerk ever since he realized that he had blown his one true chance at happiness. But now, Marcia was back in his life, and he prayed he had another chance with her.

Deep down, he sensed that she still had feelings for him, but she was touchy, sensitive, even defensive. He must not blow it this time, or he would lose her forever. He must take it slow and easy, one step at a time. A little romance, perhaps. With flowers, an elegant dinner and dancing.

Tomorrow, he would start with dinner.

CHAPTER SEVENTEEN

The next morning, Marcia was curled up on the sofa reading a fashion magazine when the phone rang. Her heart leapt to her throat. Gavin.

Her voice was deceptively disinterested when she answered the phone. "Hello."

"Marcia, please tell me you're not busy today."

Disappointed, her heart fell when she heard her agent's voice, and not Gavin's. "Hi, Michael. No, I'm not busy. Why?"

"Great. I need you to replace someone on a commercial right away. It's background work."

Background work in commercials paid well. The only problem was she didn't know when she would finish, and she'd promised to call Gavin.

Michael added, "I really need you today. You know how hard it is to replace someone last minute."

"I know." She hated to disappoint her agent. Maybe she could still get together with Gavin after the shoot. "Okay. I'll do it."

"Great, Marcia! You're a lifesaver. Call time is eleven a.m."

"Wow. It's almost ten now." She grabbed a pen and paper. "All right. Give me the details."

Michael gave her the location of the set, the description of what she needed to bring, and the name of the person she was replacing. After thanking him, she hung up and hurried to the bathroom.

A commercial would bring in hundreds of dollars, but Marcia hoped it would be a short day. Gavin wanted to see her tonight, and, despite her reservations, she was looking forward to seeing him.

"Mr. Williams," the school secretary announced over the intercom, "there's a call for you in the office."

Gavin bagged his turkey submarine sandwich and sprang to his feet. Marcia.

In the office, the secretary, said, "Line four."

Gavin went to the phone furthest from the secretary's desk. Nervousness caused his stomach to flutter "Hello?"

"Hey, man. What's up?"

His stomach calmed. It's wasn't Marcia. "Delvin. What's up?"

"Long time, no hear. Want to shoot some hoops tonight?"

"Not tonight, D. I'm busy." That wasn't exactly a lie. Although he hadn't yet heard from Marcia, he believed she would call.

"Too many papers to grade, or is it a woman?"

Gavin paused, then told another half-truth. "First year teaching is keeping me very busy."

"I hear you. But don't forget your homies. We hardly see you at the gym anymore."

"Let's hook up soon. Maybe the weekend. I'll let you know."

After disconnecting, Gavin tapped the receiver against his forehead. He had been premature in getting his hopes up. Of course Marcia wouldn't call him at work.

But would she call him at all?

Hours later, Gavin sat staring at his living room phone. He believed things had ended on a positive note yesterday, but maybe he had misinterpreted the situation. Maybe Marcia didn't want to see him again after all.

He prayed that was not the case. Earlier, anticipating an evening together, he had made reservations at an exclusive restaurant in the city.

The tick-tocking of the clock was an ever-present reminder of time passing. He called Lonita's number, but each time the answering machine picked up. Marcia must have gone out with Lonita. Finally, just after seven p.m., Gavin canceled the dinner reservations.

His friends were probably still at the gym, playing basketball or working out. It wasn't too late to meet them. Even if they weren't there, he could run a few laps around the track.

Fifteen minutes later, Gavin was in his car. He started the ignition and began backing out of the driveway. The next moment, he braked and cut the engine. He had forgotten his gym bag. As he opened his front door, he heard a faint voice upstairs. The answering machine. Taking the stairs two at a time, he charged into his bedroom. He recognized Marcia's voice.

"I was working late. If you get home any time soon—" He grabbed the receiver. "Hi there."

"Screening your calls?"

"I was on my way out."

"Oh." She sounded disappointed. "Call me when you get a chance, then."

"I'm not letting you go that easily. It figures! The moment I step out, that's when you call. I should have given you my cell number."

"I was on a set all day, and just got wrapped. Sorry I couldn't call earlier."

"That's okay."

"I was hoping—"

"So was I."

Marcia chuckled. "When will you be back home?"

"I was heading out to the gym, but if you're free—"

"I am."

In his mind, Gavin shouted, "Yes!" and was glad she couldn't see his wide, foolish grin. "Do you want to catch a late show?"

"I wouldn't mind staying in. I'm a bit tired."

His grin faded. "If you're too tired, we can get together another time."

"No." Marcia's response was quick. "I'd like to see you."

"All right. Why don't you come over here, and I'll cook dinner."

"You? Cook?"

"I make a mean Shake'n Bake™ chicken dinner with the best mac-and-cheese this side of the city."

"Sounds great, Gavin. But I'll have to take a rain check on that one."

"Why? My culinary talents don't impress you?"

"Oh, I'm quite adventurous." He could hear a smile in her voice. "But I had a late dinner on the set today."

"Too bad. I was looking forward to making a believer out of you."

"You can prove yourself another time. See you in about an hour."

Minutes after arriving at Gavin's, Marcia sat cross-legged on his sofa. "So," she began. "Tell me about your class."

One ankle crossed over the other, Gavin lounged at the opposite end of the sofa. "I'm teaching fifth grade and loving it. I've got a great group of kids. They keep me busy, though."

"Fifth grade...they must be close to puberty."

"Some have well reached that stage. I swear, some of those girls look like women."

"Any of them have a crush on you?"

"Not that I know of."

Marcia crossed her arms. "There's bound to be at least one. When I was in fourth grade—no, maybe it was third. Anyway, I had a big crush on my teacher, Mr. Poppins."

"Poppins...like Mary Poppins?"

"Yeah. He was a real sweetheart."

"Did he float around with an umbrella?"

She smiled. "Hardly. Although everyone used to ask him where he kept his umbrella. I think he was pretty sick of that joke."

"No doubt. What was so special about Mr. Poppins?"

"He was gorgeous. Tall, olive-complected. He was the best-looking teacher in the whole school, and one of the few men. I always made excuses to ask him questions, always wanted his opinion of my work. That kind of thing. It was harmless, really."

"In third grade, I would hope so. Although nowadays, kids are getting older a lot faster."

"What about you? Any teacher ever make your heart pitter-patter when you were young?"

"Not that I can remember." Gavin pursed his lips. "No, wait. I really liked my kindergarten teacher."

"So you were barely out of diapers..."

"I liked her. She was always able to make me stop crying when my mother dropped me off at class."

Marcia couldn't help giggling. "No, Gavin. Not you. My image of you is shattered."

"Hey, I got used to school. After the first few years."

They laughed, then lapsed into silence.

Gavin was the first to speak. "What commercial were you filming today?"

"A beer commercial."

"Go on. I'd like to hear about it."

"It was nothing special. I was one of about three hundred extras in a crowded bar. Dancing. Working the crowd. Enjoying the beer."

"Sounds like fun."

"It was okay. But I'm glad the day is over."

Gavin moved closer to her. "Turn around."

"What?"

He placed firm hands on her shoulder blades and guided her. "Turn your back to me. You look tense. I'll give you a massage."

"Gavin...!"

His hands kneaded her flesh. "I was right. You're tense." She wasn't prepared for Gavin touching her, wasn't prepared for the warm sensations that invaded her body.

"Just relax. Relax your shoulders. That's it."

She let go, relaxing her body, yielding to the mastery of his hands. Those strong hands, kneading and pressing the knots in her back, reminded her of their early courtship days. She missed his massages. She missed so much about him.

"You told Andrea and Lonita about Jackson?" he queried.

"Mmmhmm." She closed her eyes.

"And how did they react?"

"They're relieved that I've left him, considering what he did to me."

"Did you tell them anything about me?"

"That we're getting along." She tilted her head as Gavin's hands found a particularly tense area on her neck. "Right there. Yes. That's good."

"How did they react?"

"They just want me to be careful."

Placing her hands on his, she stopped him. He grew silent, and she could feel his warm breath caressing her neck.

She turned, facing him. "I told them not to worry because I know what I'm doing."

"Do you know what you're doing?"

"Oh, yes."

The energy between them grew electric as their gazes locked. Neither looked away. Slowly, Gavin dipped his head lower, lower, until their lips met.

Marcia's eyelids fluttered and closed. The kiss was gentle, teasing, as Gavin nipped and sucked her bottom lip softly. Trailing his fingers up her neck, he framed her face and slipped his warm tongue into her mouth. The action thrilled her, made her desperate with longing for this man.

Wrapping her arms around his neck, she arched into him, pressing her breasts against his chest. It felt good, so good to be in his arms, so good to feel his hands on her body again. She wanted him even more than she had wanted him the first time they made love.

She never should have left him. If she hadn't, maybe she would have his child right now. Maybe they would have other children. Maybe they would have realized all their goals and dreams. Her eyes misted. She fought the tears, fought the sudden feeling of depression, because she wanted this. She wanted to be with Gavin. But despite her efforts, the tears spilled down her cheeks.

Realizing something was wrong, Gavin pulled back and looked at her. He brushed away her tears. "You're not ready for this."

"I-I am."

"No, you're not."

He was right. Out of nowhere, bittersweet emotions had risen, overwhelming her.

"Hold me, Gavin."

He wrapped her in his arms, and she immediately felt secure, despite her vacillating emotions.

"I'm sorry," she whispered.

"Don't be. Make no mistake about it, Marcia. I want you. But I want you when you're ready."

Holding her close, he rocked her gently. Marcia's tense body relaxed. Gavin was a gentle, patient and loving man who cared more about pleasing her and comforting her than getting her into bed. He had always been in tune with her needs and had always put her first. That was one of the things she had loved about him.

And at this moment, she was glad to be in the arms of someone who cared about her. She was glad they were friends.

CHAPTER EIGHTEEN

The doorbell rang while Marcia was fastening her emerald earrings. Looking in the bathroom mirror, she gave herself a once-over, fluffing her loose curls and smoothing her emerald dress.

There was a knock on the bathroom door. Lonita said, "Gavin's here."

Deftly, Marcia applied dark lipstick, then stepped out of the bathroom.

"You look fabulous!" Lowering her voice, Lonita added, "He's waiting in the doorway."

"Thanks." Marcia strolled toward the vestibule. Why she was nervous she did not know.

When Gavin saw her, he whistled. Bowing, he presented her with a single red rose.

She was touched, and bent down to sniff its sweet fragrance. "Thank you, Gavin. It's beautiful."

"It pales in comparison to you."

She took in his navy pants, matching double-breasted jacket, white silk shirt, and black leather tie. At six-foot-four, he seemed larger than life. "And you look incredible."

"Thank you. Are you ready?"

He extended an arm, and she took it, calling a goodbye to Lonita.

Gavin took her to an upscale, very classy, Italian restaurant in the northern part of the city. There were marble floors and paneled walls, exquisite paintings and magnificent bronze statues. She had gone to such restaurants with Jackson since he had started working on *The Beat*, but it wasn't as much of a sacrifice or as special because Jackson could easily afford it. With Gavin, it must be a once-in-a-while treat, and she appreciated it all the more knowing he had made room for it on a teacher's budget.

Gavin stepped toward the immaculately dressed maître d'. "I have a reservation. The name's Williams."

Minutes later, they were seated at a private table for two on the upper level of the restaurant.

Marcia said, "You didn't have to bring me here. This will cost a fortune."

"Don't you worry about what it's going to cost. Nothing is too good for you."

Marcia grinned. "Thank you."

Gavin ordered an Italian white wine, the flavor rich and fruity. When it was served, he raised his glass. "I'd like to make a toast. To the recapture of happiness and love."

She met his gaze, so sincere, so loving that she felt a surge of warmth. If they weren't separated by the table's width, she would kiss him.

Slowly, deliberately, she touched her glass to his. "To happiness, Gavin. To love."

Something flowed between them, something electrifying that made her pulse race. She was sharply aware of him, the face she used to cradle in her hands, the mouth that had kissed her as no other man had ever done. His hands, his body that had loved her as no other man could ever do.

And his eyes, dark and deep, portrayed a longing as strong as her own.

Not even the arrival of dinner could break this moment of closeness. Marcia scarcely tasted her fettuccini chicken alfredo, and it was doubtful that Gavin was aware of the delicious aroma wafting from his veal parmigiana. If they broke eye contact, it was only for the briefest of moments, and was resumed immediately, like a reassuring touch they could not do without.

For dessert, they shared a piece of tiramisu. It was more than sharing a piece of cake. As they took turns feeding each other, every bite offered and every bite accepted was a shared caress.

"I want you so much," he whispered. "Are you ready to go home—my home?"

Marcia shivered. "Yes, but first—" She caught his hand, holding it tightly. "First, I must take care of some unfinished business. Come with me to Jackson's. Please? I want to get the rest of my stuff."

"My pleasure." His voice was husky. "You know what I wish? That you would take your belongings to my place."

"I...I can't decide that now."

"I understand. I won't rush you." He brushed his mouth over the hand holding his, a warm, lingering caress that sent a tingle from the tips of her fingers, up her arm and throughout her body.

"Let's go," she urged. "I want to get this over with."

Gavin settled the bill, and when they were at his car, he suggested, "We better call first. I don't want him to be home when we go there."

Marcia dialed Jackson's place on her cell. After four rings, the answering machine picked up. She disconnected. "He's not there."

They held hands as they drove to Jackson's condominium, which took twenty minutes. Marcia felt strange when she arrived at the condo, and even stranger when she stood outside the apartment door. Slowly, she inserted the key into the lock and turned it.

The place was dark and quiet. Marcia released the breath she didn't know she was holding. "He's not here. Thank goodness. I want to get my things and leave as soon as possible."

Her belongings were just as she had left them, giving the false impression that she still lived there.

Marcia went to the bedroom closet and retrieved her luggage. It took twenty minutes to pack two suitcases and a gym bag.

"Are you almost finished?" Gavin asked, forcing a suitcase shut.

"I think so. No, wait! My painting!"

She walked into the living room, and Gavin followed her. She marched right over to the painting of two white swans.

"That's yours?" Gavin asked.

"A friend painted this for me...actually for me and you, but we had broken up by the time she gave it to me." Marcia looked at Gavin and saw a of discomfort in his eyes. "Will you help me take it down?"

Gavin was helping Marcia ease the painting off the wall when they heard the apartment door open. They both turned to watch Jackson saunter into the living room. He was no less handsome than before, but Marcia no longer felt a thrill at his appearance. His good looks were only skin deep, and she had been a fool not to recognize it sooner.

Jackson's face hardened when he saw them. "What the hell is going on here?"

Gavin finished taking the painting off the wall, allowing Marcia to face Jackson.

She gave him a level stare. "I came to get the rest of my things."

"And you brought him?" Jackson asked bitterly.

"I needed someone to help me."

"Is this everything?" Gavin interjected.

Marcia nodded.

"Then let's go." Gavin handed her the picture, took the suitcases and the gym bag, and, with a disgusted look at Jackson, started for the door.

Marcia followed, but was stopped abruptly when Jackson grabbed her arm.

"Marcia, you're not going anywhere."

CHAPTER NINETEEN

"Let go of me," Marcia demanded.

Turning and seeing that Jackson had a firm grip on Marcia's arm, Gavin approached him in a menacing manner. He was taller than Jackson by at least three inches and towered over him in quite an intimidating manner.

"Let her go."

Jackson scowled up at Gavin, but released Marcia's arm. "Are you sleeping with him now, Marcia?"

Anger flared hotly, but she would not demean herself by responding to his insolence. She nudged Gavin. "Let's go."

They were almost at the door when Jackson yelled, "You're not leaving until I make sure you haven't taken anything of mine!"

"I haven't," Marcia snapped. Remembering the apartment key, she tossed it at Jackson and left.

Jackson came running into the hallway. "Marcia, wait!" Reluctantly, she turned. "What is it now?"

"You can't leave me, not like this." His demeanor had turned pathetic.

"I have already left you."

"You owe it to me—"

"I owe you nothing, Jackson. Goodbye."

"At least let me explain—"

But she turned without a word. She hurried to the elevator and pressed the down button. As the elevator doors slid open, she heard Jackson call her name. He sounded pitiful, but she did not look back. She could not. She was beginning to shake, and she didn't know if it was from relief that it was over or from guilt that she ignored his plea. Maybe she did owe him something. They'd had two years together, and most of that time had been good.

The elevator closed. Gavin, holding her suitcases and gym bag, was watching her with concern.

"I better take you to Lonita's," he said. "You look ready to drop."

She forced a smile and was about to thank him for his thoughtfulness. But then she looked into his eyes and knew it was not Lonita's comfort and solicitude she wanted—it was his. She wanted his arms around her, wanted to feel the warmth of his mouth and his hard body against hers.

"Later, you can take me to Lonita's. But first, take me to your place."

"Are you sure?" He sounded breathless. "Very sure?"

"Oh, yes." This time it took no effort at all to smile. "I'm very, very sure."

The moment they stepped in the door, Marcia wrapped her arms around Gavin's waist. "Kiss me."

He swept her into his arms. His mouth covered hers, and Marcia felt the years slip back to the time when she had been desperately in love with Gavin, when they had made love at every possible and impossible moment of every day and night. Heat flooded her body. She kissed him more urgently, molding herself against him. His arms shifted, and suddenly she was elevated as if she weighed no more than a child and carried upstairs to the bedroom.

As he lowered her onto the bed, he asked softly, "You're sure?"

In reply, she pulled him down on top of her, reveling in the feel of his strong, hard body against her softness.

Gavin pulled away. "I have to get something."

"I'm protected."

Gavin gave her a soft peck on the forehead. "That's not what I'm talking about. Just lie here."

Within minutes, he returned with a bottle of wine, and one glass. Marcia grew breathless as she saw it, the memory of its significance touching her heart. The first time they had made love, they drank wine from one glass, and then continued the tradition. Gavin had said that by doing so, they were reinforcing their love, their oneness. He'd also said that if they ever argued, this was how they should resolve the quarrel; sharing one glass would enable them to concentrate on each other and remember their love.

"Marcia."

"I know."

She took the bottle and glass from him and placed them on his dresser. Returning to him, she pulled him into an embrace. "Oh, Gavin, I know."

He framed her face with his hands and gazed at her. The caring she saw in his eyes warmed her soul. Four years seemed like four hours. This was how they were meant to be—in each other's arms, loving each other.

He kissed her forehead, each eyelid, her nose, her chin. Marcia didn't breathe. Slowly, his mouth came down on hers, and she parted her lips with a soft moan. A flame erupted deep in her belly, spreading quickly to the rest of her body. Arching into him, she slipped her arms around his neck.

It felt so good to be back in his arms. Her fingers explored his shoulders, remembering, enjoying. How she wanted him now, needed him. She needed to join with him body-to-body, soul-to-soul.

Gavin deepened the kiss and pulled her down with him onto the bed. One hand caressed her back while the other found her zipper and undid it. He nudged the material off her shoulders and feathered kisses from her shoulder to the soft curve of her breast.

Marcia drew in a sharp breath. His kisses were driving her delirious, making her light-headed, as they had the first time he had shown her the depth of his love. How exquisite it would be to have him inside her again after all this time. Her nipples hardened at the thought.

Slipping her dress to her waist, Gavin traced the delicate material of her bra with his fingertips. Marcia brought her hand to his cheek and gently stroked the smooth flesh.

Gavin unclasped her bra. His mouth caressed one nipple, his fingers the other. She arched her back wantonly.

"Gavin," she whispered, her voice hoarse with longing. "You're driving me crazy."

"No more than you drive me crazy."

He turned her over and brushed her hair aside. His breath was hot against the back of her neck as he skimmed his lips against her flesh. Then, pulling her onto her knees, he entered her from behind. He filled her totally, completely, reaching a place deep inside her that sent wave after tingling wave of pleasure through her body with each deepening thrust of his swollen member. She was aflame with longing, arching against him, learning his rhythm again and moving faster, faster, until a tidal wave of pleasure spiraled in her. Gripping the sheets, she cried out.

Gavin's climax came shortly after, and he gripped Marcia tightly as he let out a long, rapturous moan. For several seconds he held her, nestling himself deep inside her as he succumbed to his release. After his spasms subsided, he lay beside her and cradled her in his arms.

His mouth captured hers in a hungry, breathless kiss. "It's been so long, Marcia. I missed you so much."

"Me too." Until now, she hadn't realized how much.

Gavin trailed his hand down her belly to her most sensitive spot. Marcia whimpered as he played with her delicately, teasing her. She wrapped an arm around his waist, drawing him closer.

This time, he loved her gently, slowly. Marcia's second climax was even more forceful than the first, and she knew she had found heaven on earth.

Gavin climaxed, crying out her name. She held him tightly and smiled when he collapsed against her. It was wonderful to have this closeness again, their bodies touching, their breaths mingling at this precious moment just after making love.

It had been too long, indeed.

CHAPTER TWENTY

The following week, Marcia was on the set from Monday to Friday, twelve hours each day. She missed Gavin terribly, but there was no time to see him; she hardly had time to speak to him on the phone. Even though she was enjoying the work, and even though hers was a fairly important role in the film and could give her the exposure she needed to put her career back into high gear, she prayed for the weekend to come.

Finally, it was Friday, the last day of the shoot. The day had been going very well, and the production was actually ahead of schedule. Next to shoot was a scene in the office, where the lawyers discussed the fact that the FBI had come to visit them. The senior partners in the firm wanted to make sure that everyone was in agreement—to keep their mouths shut.

Marcia's character, Mary Wiles, was supposed to agree, then leave the room hastily. A senior partner would notice her departure and follow her out. He would catch up with her in the underground parking lot.

This was the scene Marcia had been looking forward to shooting, as her character got killed by the senior partner. Although Mary Wiles appeared strong, the lawyers feared she would be a weak link and had decided to silence her permanently..

Marcia and the other actors rehearsed the meeting scene several times until the director felt that they had gotten it right.

The lighting director tested and set up the appropriate lights to make it appear as if daylight was streaming through the blinds, which was impossible to accomplish naturally, since they were in a darkened studio. The magic of filmmaking never ceased to enthrall Marcia, and she loved being a part of it.

"All right, let's shoot this," shouted the director.

The cinematographer and camera assistants hustled frantically. Hair, makeup, and wardrobe personnel fussed around the actors. The assistant directors communicated via walkie-talkies. Finally, everything was ready.

It took eleven takes before the director and cinematographer were satisfied. Filmmaking was often tedious, but Marcia loved it with a passion only others in the film industry could understand.

"You'll have about half-an-hour before we need you again, Marcia," an assistant director told her.

"Thanks." Half an hour most likely meant an hour-and-a-half. So she made her way to her spacious

Winnebago™, equipped with everything she needed. There was a large mirror and counter, a toilet and sink, a plush sofa which doubled as a bed, and even a television.

Marcia made herself comfortable on the sofa, stretching her slim body across its full length. She yawned and closed her eyes, but immediately bolted upright. If she fell asleep now, she would want to sleep for hours and might end up more fatigued than energized.

She decided to call Gavin from her cell phone. It was a little after five-thirty, and he should be home. But he did not answer. Marcia felt a nagging disappointment. She had been looking forward to hearing his voice.

She called Lonita.

Lonita answered in a deep, seductive voice. "Hello?"

"It's only me," Marcia said. "Not tall, dark, and handsome."

Lonita's tone instantly changed to its normal, somewhat high-pitched caliber. "What's up, girlfriend?"

"Any calls for me?"

"You mean any calls from Gavin."

Marcia smiled. "Since you mention it…"

"Not today. He knows you're on the set, doesn't he?"

"Yes." Marcia was disappointed. "You're right. I'll call him later."

"You know, I'm still waiting to hear the scoop...about you and Gavin. You're being very secretive about this one."

"You know we're trying to work things out."

"But I don't know how you feel. With everything that happened with Jackson..."

"Jackson is my past."

"You said that about Gavin once."

"True. But the circumstances were different. Anyway, there are no guarantees things will work out for us."

"Just make sure you get past the past. That's the only way."

That thought disturbed Marcia. More than once she had questioned whether or not she could truly have a relationship with Gavin without telling him about the baby...and her other secret. But how could she? Not only would he hate her for not telling him about the baby, the pain was still too great. Perhaps it always would be. She had never shared her secrets with anyone, not even her sister and best friend.

"I do hope you work it out. You deserve some happiness."

"I hope so, too."

"Andrea's here. She's anxious to speak with you."

"This isn't about Curtis, I hope."

"No. Jackson."

That piqued Marcia's curiosity. Seconds later, Andrea came to the phone.

"Sis," Andrea began, "have you called Jackson lately?"

"No."

"Well, he keeps calling me. He's determined to find out where you are."

"You told him what I said?" Marcia asked.

"Yes," Andrea replied. "But he doesn't believe that you're vacationing down South."

Marcia chewed on her bottom lip. "I suppose I'll have to call him sometime...to tell him to stop harassing the people I care about. Andrea, I've got to run. Tell Lonita I might not be home until tomorrow."

"Oooh. Spending the night with Gavin?"

"Maybe." She hoped.

"Tell him I said hi. And don't do anything that I wouldn't do." Andrea giggled.

Her sister never failed to make Marcia smile. She flipped her phone closed, then reopened it. Once more, she dialed Gavin's number.

Still no answer.

When the last child had left for home, Gavin knocked on J.P.'s door. "You still working? And you call me a workaholic."

J.P. rose from his desk and stretched. "Not anymore. Hey, what's up with you? Nowadays you're here till four, then you rush off."

"Why don't we go for dinner, and I'll tell you about it."

Half-an-hour later, Gavin and J.P. were seated in a booth at their favorite steak house. Gavin ordered a T-bone steak with sautéed mushrooms and potatoes, and J.P. ordered a salmon steak with rice.

"Now," said J.P. "What's going on? You've had a grin glued to your face this last week and you've been walking on air. Everyone, and I mean everyone, is wondering what happened to you."

"Are you saying that I'm not ordinarily a happy kind of guy?"

J.P. raised his brows.

"So, it's obvious that something has happened?" asked Gavin, smiling from ear-to-ear.

"Is your skin brown?" J.P. smirked. "Enough with the secrecy, Williams. Spit it out."

"Do you remember the woman I told you about? The one I was engaged to years ago?"

J.P. nodded.

"Well, we're back together."

"When did that happen?" J.P. did not try to hide his surprise. "After what you told me, I didn't think you two would work things out this soon."

"Neither did I, but something happened that worked in my favor." Gavin explained about Marcia and Jackson, how she had come to him for comfort.

"And now she loves you again, just like that?"

Gavin hesitated. "She hasn't said it. But yes, I'm sure she loves me."

"Are you sure she's ready for this? I mean, she just ended what you said was a long-term relationship. Maybe she's on the rebound."

Gavin hadn't really thought about that—he hadn't wanted to. He loved Marcia and all he had wanted was for them to be back together.

"I think she was on the rebound from me when she met him."

"I hope you're right."

"I am."

"Thanks, Chris. See you again." Marcia waved at the second assistant director as she made her way to the parking lot. It was after nine-thirty, and she was finished filming. When she reached her car, she leaned against it and retrieved her cell phone from her purse. Before heading to Lonita's, she would try Gavin again.

This time, he answered. Pleasantly surprised, Marcia said, "You're home."

"Marcia. Man, am I happy to hear your voice."

"Feel like company?"

"Only if it's you."

"I'm on my way."

Thirty minutes later, Gavin welcomed her in his muscular arms. "I missed you, Marcia."

"It's been a long week."

"And you're finished? Completely?"

"Yes, but I might have to go back in and reshoot any shots that didn't turn out right."

"When?"

"Whenever they call me. I might not have to."

Gavin bent and kissed her. Just one simple kiss, yet her head was spinning. It was amazing the effect this man had on her.

She whispered, "Make love to me."

Gavin swept her into his arms, kissing her as he carried her upstairs to the bedroom. They had made love hundreds of times, yet every time he touched her it was as exciting as the first time they had been lovers.

Nudging the bedroom door open with his shoulder, he carried her over the threshold and laid her on the bed. She pulled him against her, wrapping her arms tightly around his well-toned back. One week away from him had been too long.

Their gazes met and held as he unbuttoned her blouse, then unclasped her bra. As potent as any caress, his eyes roamed her body, enchanting her as only he could. Biting down on his lower lip, he trailed a finger along her throat, through the valley of her breasts, over her midriff and into her belly button, then to her skirt waist. He skimmed it and her panties over her hips.

His mouth was so close to her, she felt the heat of his breath. Slowly, deliberately, he brought his tongue down onto her most private spot. As he teased her, loved her, she felt the first tingling sensations hit her, the sweetest of sensations that only Gavin could make her feel. Whispering his name, she arched against the tantalizing pressure of his tongue until the pulsing and throbbing of her pleasure point became an engulfing flame that spread through her body.

"Gavin. Gavin." She cried his name over and over as her body was rocked by spasms she couldn't restrain. She was taken to another time, another place, a place so magical she didn't want to leave.

Gavin ran his tongue along her searing flesh from her navel to her lips, then kissed her with a passion that ignited a heated response. She unfastened his pants, pulling them off with his underwear, her hands tracing the taut muscles of his thighs.

Gavin's breath was ragged and his eyes were hot and hungry as he lowered himself, then thrust his arousal deep inside her.

She gripped his buttocks and held him tightly as she welcomed the first pleasurable thrusts. Faster and faster he moved. He loved her wildly, savagely, the way only a man who had been denied too long could love. Deep inside her, the heat of pleasure rekindled. She wrapped her legs around his slick hips, feeling him go deeper and faster until she could think of nothing but the pulsing tension building in her. Building, and then exploding.

"Gavin!" she cried as she was once more shaken by spasms of pleasure.

"Yes, my love. Yes!" He thrust again and again, his body taut as he savored his own release.

He collapsed against her, and she held him close. Only Gavin could make her feel this good, this loved.

"I love you, Marcia," he said. "I always have, and I always will."

She lay very still, hardly daring to breathe. This was when she should assure him that she loved him, too. And she did, didn't she? She would have hardly entered into another relationship with him otherwise.

But she had been wrong before. She'd made so many mistakes. Suddenly, she was very frightened of making another one.

"Gavin, I need—"

He stopped her with a kiss. "Don't say another word. I've rushed you. I've hardly had enough time to prove that I'm no longer the fool who was intimidated by your career. Give me a chance, Marcia. Let me date you. Prove myself."

She gazed into his eyes, so sincere, so compelling. "Yes, Gavin."

"Then let me start by inviting you to meet my mother. Again."

CHAPTER TWENTY-ONE

The very next day, Saturday, Gavin drove Marcia to see his mother. They were almost there, and suddenly he was as nervous as a schoolboy taking his first date home.

"I told her only that I'd be coming to dinner," he said as he turned into the tree-shaded street where his family had lived for eighteen years. "That I'd have a surprise for her."

"What?" cried Marcia. "You didn't warn her about me?"

He glanced at her briefly. How lovely she was, eyes wide with indignation and, perhaps a hint of apprehension. She had her hair drawn back in a simple ponytail, wore just a trace of dark lipstick on her gorgeous mouth, and a brown knit top that hugged her curves.

"Don't worry," he said. "I did tell her that I am seeing you again. She said she's glad. She'd always hoped we'd get back together."

Turning the steering wheel, he maneuvered the car into the driveway of his mother's home. As she always did, Mrs. Williams was peering through the curtains, anxiously awaiting her son's arrival.

When they stepped up to the door, Mrs. Williams already had it wide open. Gavin went straight into her arms, hugging her heartily.

"Hey, Mama," he said when he released her. "How are you feeling today?"

"Not too bad at all, son. Just a little tired."

Marcia stepped forward. "Hello, Mrs. Williams."

Cicely Williams' face lit in a wide smile. "Come here, you," she said to Marcia, then pulled her into a warm embrace. "I'm so happy to see you!"

"So am I." Marcia returned the heavy-set woman's hug. "Gavin told me about…the cancer. Are you okay? Really?"

"I'm alive, and that's a lot to be thankful for." Cicely Williams released Marcia. "You two come on in. Angela is in the living room."

Gavin's younger sister, in gray sweat pants and a black hooded top, lounged on the sofa with a book in her hand. She looked tired, but was still as beautiful as Marcia remembered, with her hair cut short in a cute bob. Angela's eyes lit up when she saw her brother.

Gavin dropped onto the sofa and planted a kiss on her cheek. "Don't tell me you're studying."

Angela gave him a playful nudge. "My last chance, brother dear. I need great marks if I want to get into law school."

Ever since their brother Marcus had been killed, Angela had concentrated on becoming a lawyer. She believed that society needed more minority lawyers to make sure that justice prevailed for all.

"Hey, Angela," Marcia said.

"What a surprise!" Angela rose to wrap her arms around Marcia. "Good to see you again."

Marcia's eyes misted. Everyone was so kind, so loving. Not that she expected hostility from Gavin's family, but naturally, they must have blamed her just a little for the breakup.

Mrs. Williams took a seat in the love seat adjacent to the sofa. "Now, I may be getting old and all that, but it looks to me like you two…are you two back together?"

Gavin met and held Marcia's gaze. "Actually, we're dating. I'm trying to convince her that we belong together."

Mrs. Williams squealed. "I was hoping…I know you both will work things out."

"So do I," added Angela. "You two were so in love. A love like that never dies."

That's what Gavin was counting on. If he and Marcia could finally close the door on the negative chapter in their lives, they had a chance at a future.

Mrs. Williams rose. "This is the oldest cliché in the book, but complete honesty is the only way. Without it, you have nothing."

Marcia watched as Gavin's mother disappeared into the kitchen. The uneasy feeling had rushed back. She wanted a future with Gavin, but could she risk it? Could she tell him the truth? He might reject her, hurt her. And her heart could not handle any more pain.

Gavin reached for her hand, but she folded her arms before he could take it in his. "Do you need any help, Mrs. Williams?" she called loudly.

"No, dear," came her reply. "You just sit down and relax."

The dinner was ready within fifteen minutes, and Gavin, Marcia, Angela, and Mrs. Williams settled themselves at the table. Mrs. Williams graced the table before they partook of the meal.

Sitting here with his family and the woman he loved, Gavin's heart felt full. He had made the right decision to bring Marcia here. His mother had always loved her as a daughter and had been crushed when their relationship ended.

In the back of his mind, the threat that his mother might die was very real. The doctors said she was very lucky, since the cancer had been caught early. Gavin couldn't call being diagnosed with cancer "lucky," but he had to concede that she had been fortunate to discover the lump when she had. Still, she'd had to endure chemotherapy and radiation treatments, which had caused hair loss and severe nausea.

Now, her sparse gray hair had grown back, and she had regained the weight she'd lost. Thank God she was healthy and happy. She was the only parent Gavin had ever truly known, and he wanted to protect her and keep her around for as long as possible.

Gavin drew in a deep breath. He knew his mother wouldn't live forever, and the thought of the cancer returning—which was a possibility even though she was in remission—scared him more than he cared to admit. He glanced at Marcia, who was munching on a roll, then surprised her with a spontaneous kiss on the temple.

She glanced at him quizzically. "What was that for?"

"Just because." Because he didn't want to waste any more time. Because he wanted to spend the rest of his life with her.

Marcia smiled appreciatively, then turned back to her food. He loved her smile.

After dinner, Cicely Williams brought dessert to the table. Gavin rubbed his palms together. "Mmmm, apple pie."

Cutting an extra-large piece, his mother gave him an affectionate look. "And you'll no doubt want ice cream?"

"Sure, Mama. If you've got vanilla."

The evening passed quickly with conversation and laughter. Gavin was sorry when it was time for him and Marcia to leave.

"Mama," Gavin said as he stood in the doorway, "I had a great time tonight."

Mrs. Williams embraced him. "I love you, son. Drive carefully." She turned to Marcia and hugged her, too. "You two come by as often as you like. With Angela studying so much, I do get lonely."

"We'll be back, Mrs. Williams," Marcia assured her. She winked. "Even if it's only to make sure Gavin's belly is full."

Laughter accompanied their final goodbyes. As Gavin backed out of the driveway, he could see his mother's smiling face in the brightly lit window. He tooted the horn as he drove off into the darkness.

He glanced at Marcia beside him, but she was already asleep. His wristwatch showed it was after ten p.m., later than he had thought.

Gavin smiled to himself. The afternoon and evening had been great. His mother had accepted Marcia back into her life wholeheartedly, which would make things a lot easier since he was planning a future with this woman.

A future…marriage…a house full of children.

The thought made Gavin tingle all over. He was an old-fashioned kind of guy with old-fashioned values. Losing his brother and almost losing his mother had reinforced for him the importance of family. He wanted a family with Marcia.

But as much as he wanted to ask her to marry him, it was too soon. He couldn't forget how she had tensed when he told her that he loved her.

He would wait a little longer. He must not scare her off by moving too fast.

CHAPTER TWENTY-TWO

For the next several weeks, Marcia was extremely busy. She'd landed various commercials and two small parts in television movies. Work was better than it had been in a very long time, and she was glad. But with steady work came long hours, and long hours meant less time to spend with Gavin.

Despite the fact that they saw each other only once or twice a week, they were getting very close again, almost as close as they had been before. More than four years earlier, Marcia had barely survived the breakup. Never in a million years had she believed that she and Gavin would find their way back to each other. But they had.

And she hadn't been haunted by any dreams lately. Finally, she had made peace with herself and with her past.

Although Jackson continued to page her, and continued to call her and her sister trying to reach her, Marcia did not call him. There was no point. Sooner or later, he would realize that their relationship was irrevocably over. At least she'd had the good fortune of not running into him.

Her parents, especially her mother, had welcomed Gavin back with open arms. Just as Gavin's family had welcomed her.

Without a doubt, things were looking up for her.

Earlier today, Gavin had called her from school and told her not to make any plans for dinner. He was going to treat her. Again.

He had been wonderfully romantic on several occasions, romancing her under the moonlight with a bottle of wine and music. Maybe because they weren't able to spend much time together, Gavin made the times when they did meet exciting and memorable. Not that she needed wine or music or fancy dinners. He was enough. He made her feel giddy and head-over-heels, just the way she had felt when she'd first met him.

Maybe because she was looking forward to this evening that they were going to share, the hours passed slowly. When she later arrived at his home, and he opened the door for her, she fell into his arms. "I missed you."

Gavin ran his hands through her hair, then framed her face gently. Her lips parted in soft invitation, an invitation Gavin accepted. His mouth captured hers in a sweet, gentle kiss, a tender kiss that conveyed the depth of his affection for her. He nipped and sucked gently, and Marcia felt such contentment, such warmth...she could stay there with him like that for eternity.

The kiss grew more urgent, and Gavin wrapped his arms tightly around her. They were going to make love—again. Again, like they had every stolen moment they shared. Again, before they'd had a chance to eat dinner. Again, because a simple kiss was enough to ignite a burning passion. They were like two young lovers, insatiable, never getting enough of each other.

That thought caused Marcia to grin against Gavin's lips, and her grin soon turned to a giggle.

He pulled away from her and stared deeply into her eyes. "What's so funny?"

"Us. The way we can't get enough of each other."

Gavin cocked an eyebrow. "And that's a problem?"

"Not at all." She trailed a fingertip across his jaw and over his lips. "It's only an observation."

He took her finger into his mouth and sucked softly. The simple act was utterly erotic, and Marcia's eyelids fluttered shut as she delighted in the arousing sensation. He scooped her into his arms and carried her to the bedroom, then gently laid her on the bed.

Their coupling was wild, wonderful, and magical. It took them to the special place their passion always brought them, a place of warmth where time was suspended and there was only each other. When they climaxed, they clung to each other, bodies entwined as well as their hearts.

A little while later, Marcia rolled over onto her side. If she didn't get up now, they would spend the rest of the evening in bed.

Hmmm, Marcia thought. *That's not such a bad idea.*

She sat upright. It *was* a bad idea. The evening was still young, and they should enjoy it in other ways.

"Are we going out for dinner?" she asked. She cast a glance at Gavin, who was just opening his eyes. "You told me not to cook, because you wanted to treat me."

Gavin sat up and stretched. "I wish we could just stay in bed."

Marcia ran a finger along his brawny chest. Her tone was playful when she asked, "This relationship isn't a strictly sexual one for you, is it, Gavin Williams?"

He swept her into his arms, nuzzling her neck with his nose. "You only wish."

She burst into laughter. "Your sexual appetite is insatiable, you know that?"

"And you love it." He gave her a chaste kiss, not at all like what she expected. "All right. Get dressed. My surprise will be here shortly."

He bounced off of the bed, his firm, naked buttocks the last she saw of him before he disappeared into the bathroom.

The surprise was coming. What could that mean?

She would have joined Gavin in the shower, except she knew what the result would be. So instead, she waited patiently until Gavin was finished before she indulged in a long, cool shower of her own.

Wrapped in a large white towel, she stepped out of the bathroom—and couldn't believe her eyes. There were candles everywhere, on the floor outlining the hallway, and on each step down to the main level.

Marcia followed their path. In the living room, candles glowed softly on the coffee table, the television, and the end tables. In the dining room, where Gavin was waiting, two white candles illuminated the beautifully set dining table. Candles provided the only light in the entire place, and they created a most beautiful, romantic aura.

"Gavin—" She all but squealed with delight. "What is all this?"

"You better get dressed. You can't eat dinner in a towel."

With a last curious look at the dining table, where champagne was chilling and two silver covers hid the plates beneath, she scurried back upstairs to the bedroom. Clad in a simple gray dress, she returned to the dining room in a very few minutes.

Gavin seated her with a great show of ceremony.

"Goodness, Gavin. When did you have the time to do all this?"

"Oh," he replied mysteriously, "I have my ways."

Marcia looked in awe at the magnificent setup. He'd obviously had it catered, which was nothing short of miraculous since she'd only been in the shower fifteen minutes. "How…when…?"

"Am I the man or what?"

Marcia flashed him a smile. "You are definitely the man. And you must have some serious romancing in mind."

Gavin lifted the silver covers, revealing a delicious looking meal of sautéed chicken breast, rice pilaf, and baby carrots, then took a seat opposite her.

"I'm sorry," he said, rising again. "I forgot to give you champagne."

He struggled briefly with the cork before there was a satisfying pop. The champagne fizzed and bubbled, and Marcia quickly raised a delicate crystal flute to catch the precious liquid.

"Are we celebrating something?" she asked.

"Us." Gavin filled his own glass. "May we always be as happy as we are now."

"To us." Marcia leaned forward and lightly clinked her glass against Gavin's. She tasted the liquid, which was dry and tingled in her mouth. She met Gavin's gaze, warm, tender, loving. It was like a wonderful dream. She was basking in the attentive care of this very special man. She was happy.

But didn't all dreams come to an end?

Taking another sip of the champagne, she pushed the irksome thought to the back of her mind. She was happy now, happier than she'd ever been, and she didn't want anything to spoil that.

"I've been thinking," Gavin suddenly said, drawing Marcia's attention from her plate to his gleaming dark eyes. "About what you said earlier."

"What was that?"

"You asked if this relationship was only sexual for me—"

"I was kidding," Marcia quickly interjected.

"I know. But whether or not you meant to, you touched on a topic I've been thinking about for a long time."

"What topic?"

He took her hand. "Things have been going wonderfully for us, as wonderful as the first time—if that's possible." His eyes suddenly clouded with concern as he stared at her. "You're happy, aren't you, Marcia?"

"Very happy."

"Good. Because I've never been happier. And I was thinking it's time we talked about marriage."

Her fork dropped from her hand, clattering against the plate. "You want to get married?"

"Yes. Don't you?"

"I know things have been going well, but...marriage?"

"You trust me, don't you?"

She met his gaze. "Yes."

"You know I'm not the same fool I once was. I accept you, your career, everything about you."

"I don't know if I'm ready for that kind of commitment." She averted her eyes. "I...so much has happened."

Gavin squeezed her hand. "Marcia, I'll never hurt you again. I promise you."

She whispered, "I'm afraid, Gavin. This is all moving so fast."

"We don't have to set the date right away. We can be engaged for a while."

"We were engaged before. It didn't work out."

"I know." He rubbed his thumb across her hand. "But we're more mature than we were the first time around."

"It hurt, Gavin. It hurt so much when we broke up. Then Jackson...I've made a lot of mistakes."

"It's different now. We've worked things out."

Not everything. But he couldn't know that. Could they really have a future without complete honesty?

Gavin lightly touched her face. "Look at me. I haven't been wrong all this time, have I? That was the whole point of this dating again—to move toward a greater commitment?"

"Yes."

"Good, because I love you, Marcia. And I want to marry you and have a house full of children."

Marcia felt a cold chill wash over her.

"I'm willing to wait until you're ready, but let's get engaged now. Give me something to look forward to."

Children? He wanted a house full of children?

The reality of him bringing up the mere idea horrified her. How could she handle getting pregnant—again? There was no way.

"Marcia." Gavin's voice deepened with concern. "What's wrong? You have this strange look on your face."

"No."

"No, what? You don't want to have children?"

"No." She shook her head vehemently. "I-I won't"

Abruptly, she rose and walked over to the window, wrapping her arms around her torso. Behind her back she heard the sound of his chair pushing back on the hardwood floor.

"I don't understand, Marcia." He was coming closer. "You always wanted children."

She shivered. She didn't want him near her. Not now.

"You told me. Don't you remember?" He stood so close that his breath fanned the back of her head. "When we got engaged, the first thing you said was that you were looking forward to having our babies."

"No!" She spun, pushing him back with all the force she could muster. "I can't, Gavin! I can't and I won't go through that again."

CHAPTER TWENTY-THREE

Gavin stood, stunned. "What do you mean you can't go through that *again?*"

Overcome by painful memories, Marcia hardly heard him. Her baby…their baby. Dead.

"Answer me, Marcia. What do you mean you can't go through that again?"

He was insistent. And she hadn't even meant to say that. Never had she planned to tell Gavin what had happened to her in Vancouver.

"Why do you need to know, Gavin?" Memories of the pain consumed her, and that was all she could feel. Not the love they had shared, not the intimate moments, not the passion.

"You didn't care what happened when you turned your back on me four years ago. It can hardly matter to you now."

He looked baffled. "I don't understand."

"No, you don't. You never have, and you never will." Gavin reached out to touch her face, but she pulled away. "Please leave me alone," Marcia managed to say, her voice hoarse with emotion.

"I can't do that." He clasped her arm. "Don't shake me off, Marcia! We need to talk."

Their eyes met and held, hers misting with tears. Here was Gavin, who had offered her friendship and comfort when Jackson hurt her. Who made her feel wonderful and desirable. And he was the man who had inflicted the deepest pain ever. He had hurt her once, and despite his sweet words, his wonderful surprises, his love for her, he could hurt her again.

Her dream had come to a bitter end.

"Gavin, I can't marry you."

His face turned ashen. "Why not? I love you, Marcia. For heaven's sake, is my love not enough for you?"

"I won't love you again. I can't, Gavin." It hurt to say this, but if her heart was breaking, surely it was over the tragedy of her past. "Let me go, Gavin. I'm leaving now."

His grip tightened as he stared at her as if he was trying to look deep into her soul.

"You're shaking." Slowly, still looking as if he had received a blow to the gut, he let go of her arm. "I won't force you to stay and explain, but I wish you would trust me—even if you can't love me."

She turned without a word. Her purse was on the coffee table in the living room. She snatched it, snuffing one of the candles and making others flicker with her jerky movements.

"At least let me drive you." Gavin appeared beside her, his face so pinched, his eyes so dull and lifeless that she couldn't bear to look at him.

She shook her head. "I want to be alone."

As she let herself out, she heard him call, "I'm not giving up, Marcia! I still love you!"

For one fleeting moment she was tempted to stay, to turn around and take him in her arms, to believe in fairy tales.

But she didn't. Leaving was the only option. Their relationship was over.

Gavin slumped onto the sofa. What the hell had just happened?

One minute Marcia had been smiling at him and toasting their happiness. The next, she gave him a blow equaled only by the pain of their breakup four years ago.

He must have said something…something that scared her.

Marriage. He'd talked about marriage.

And children.

She'd been okay when he mentioned that they should consider marriage. It was only later, when he mentioned children…she had looked as if she were seeing a ghost. But why?

What couldn't she go through again? Loving him and losing him? Was she afraid he would once more demand she give up her career for him—and the children they would have?

No. She must know that he was no longer the fool he was years ago. She must know that he loved her, that he would respect her career as he respected his own.

But she didn't.

He sat up, clapping a hand to his throbbing head. He was a fool still. A bigger fool than before. He never assured her that he would help her manage a career and a family. And she needed that assurance. Somehow, he must convince her.

CHAPTER TWENTY-FOUR

Marcia drove, shaking, crying, remembering. Remembering the joy, the pain, of four and a half years ago…

"You're pregnant."

Marcia held her breath as she looked at her doctor. "Are you sure?"

Dr. Kurt Jennings, her physician for several years, smiled. "Absolutely. Just about two months, it looks like."

After the third consecutive day of vomiting, Marcia had decided to go to the doctor. She felt awful all day—not just in the morning—which was why she had first assumed that she had the flu. But when she noticed that she didn't have the usual symptoms associated with the flu—fever, fatigue, and a general feeling of being run down—she had begun to wonder if she indeed had a life growing inside her.

She left the doctor's office and rushed to the nearest pay phone. She wanted to tell Gavin the good news right away. She always knew that they would have a life together, and what a blessing to be pregnant with his child!

On the way to the phone, she fantasized that she knew the exact moment of conception. It was the night of that terrible rainstorm a couple months ago that had washed out some roads. Gavin had arrived at her apartment soaking wet. He'd been shivering from cold, and she had helped him out of his clothes. He had helped her out of hers. That night, when they made love, they had climaxed at the exact moment. And as they had settled into a comfortable embrace, Marcia had felt the most unique, pleasant aura. Instinctively, she'd touched her belly. And now she knew that her instincts had been correct.

Disappointed, she hung up the phone after letting it ring about ten times. Gavin wasn't home. She would just have to wait until she saw him later. She couldn't wait to see the expression on his face when he learned he was going to be a father.

The moment she got home, she checked her answering machine. There were two messages from her agent, saying to call him right away. Her breath caught. This could be the call she'd been waiting for. Her excitement building, she dialed her agent's number.

"Michael?" she said anxiously when he answered the phone. "It's Marcia."

"Congratulations! You got the part. The producers absolutely loved you. They said you were their only choice."

She let out a squeal of delight. "Please tell me you're not kidding..."

"All right. I'm telling you." She could hear his smile through the phone. "You got the part of Jenny. The lead role. Congratulations, kid."

When she ended the call with Michael, she jumped a foot in the air, screaming ecstatically. She got the part! This was her big break, what she had been waiting for, praying for. The part of Jenny Winters—a young nurse at a medical center—was a dream role. Steady work on a television series! What more could she ask for as an actress? And as one of the show's main leads to boot! She could almost die from the excitement. Out of a cross-country casting call, she had landed the role!

She could hardly contain her delight, and when Gavin finally called, she was brief, telling him only that he needed to get over to her place right away because she had great news to tell him.

Half-an-hour later, Gavin was at her door. Marcia greeted him with a long kiss.

He broke the kiss and said, "You sounded pretty excited over the phone. What's going on?"

Taking his hand, Marcia led him to the living room. "Oh, I have such good news. Two items of good news! Which do you want to hear first?"

"How would I know?' Gavin asked, now equally caught up in her excitement "I've got no idea what you're going to tell me. Just tell me something."

She sat on the sofa and pulled him down beside her. "Remember that audition I went to last week?"

"The nurse role. You were really hyped about it"

"That's the one. Well, guess what? I talked to my agent today and I got the part! I've got one of the lead roles!" She threw her arms around Gavin's neck and hugged him tightly. "This is so wonderful, I can't believe it!"

"That's great" He broke the hug and looked at her, his eyes narrowed. "But aren't you going to have to relocate to Vancouver for that show?"

"You mean *we,* Gavin. Yes! Oh my God, this is so exciting I can hardly stand it!"

It took Marcia about a minute to realize that Gavin was not rejoicing. Sensing something was terribly wrong, her smile faded. "Gavin...what is it?"

He shrugged and diverted his gaze. "Are you going to accept the part?"

"What kind of question is that? Of course I'm going to take it."

"What about us?"

Marcia felt light-headed as she looked at him. "What do you mean?"

"I can't go to Vancouver."

"What do you mean, you can't go? It'll be great. You don't have a permanent teaching job, and I've heard there are a number of opportunities for new teachers in British Columbia. And while you're looking for a job, I can support us both—"

"No."

"Why not? Do you know how much money I'm going to be making?"

"That doesn't matter, Marcia."

"Of course it matters. Hey, you won't even have to work if you don't want to."

"When we move in together, I want us to be planning a future. How can we be planning a future when you're running all over the country with various jobs?"

Stunned, Marcia stared at Gavin for several moments. Finally, she reached out and cupped his chin, turning his face so that he had to look at her.

"Maybe I didn't make myself clear. This is a regular gig, a regular role. It could last years."

"All my family is here. I can't leave them."

Her heart plummeted, spiraling down to the depths of misery. "I don't understand."

"You know how much my family means to me."

"Of course I do. But people leave their families all the time. Start their own families..."

Gavin took her hand from his face and placed it in her lap. Silent alarm bells went off. This was not supposed to be happening.

He said, "I can't leave my mother and my baby sister. Not after Marcus. I just can't do it."

"I know how much it hurt when Marcus died. But we can start our own family. I love you, Gavin."

"Then don't go."

She cringed. He couldn't be asking her this. Not when he knew how important her career was to her. "Gavin, why are you saying this?"

"I've never understood why you've been so obsessed with being an actress."

"Because I love it!"

"Why can't you just get a normal job like everyone else? A job where you won't have to move all the time. Now, it's Vancouver. What next? Hollywood? I can't live in Hollywood. That's no place to raise a family."

"You've never objected before. Why now?"

"Because—" His mouth tightened.

"Because now I'm actually realizing a goal? Is that it? You never expected me to succeed, did you? You expected me to what? Keep getting small parts, keep going to auditions and then eventually burn out?"

He looked away.

"I'm right, aren't I? Is that why you stayed with me this long—because you expected me to eventually burn out and give up this business?"

"Marcia, I thought you knew what I wanted when I proposed to you. I've always told you how important it is for me to be close to my family—physically."

"And I thought that you knew what I wanted—what I was about. I've never been a flake; acting is my passion. This is the role of a lifetime. An opportunity like this may never come along again."

"Then you've got a tough decision to make. Let me know what you decide." He rose from the sofa and walked to the door.

Stunned beyond words, Marcia sat stock-still. She hadn't even had a chance to tell him the best news. But this was not the time. Maybe when he had calmed down and was thinking rationally.

"Gavin, where are you going?"

He faced her, his expression blank. "I'm giving you some time alone. I don't want to influence your decision."

She flew to him, grabbing his arm. "You can't just walk out! This doesn't make any sense. I thought you loved me."

"Marcia," he said softly. "You're being unfair. You can't expect me to run off to Vancouver."

"What about me? Could you stand to lose me like that? You wouldn't even fight for me, for this love we've shared for three years?"

"If our love means anything to you, you won't go."

Marcia could only stare at him. This was not the man she had known and loved for three precious years of her life. The man who had whispered words of love to her, who had made her feel like a queen. This man was a stranger.

"You can't ask me not to go. Gavin, if you love me, you must know that."

His face was taut. "This is getting us nowhere. Let's talk tomorrow."

Marcia pressed a hand to her mouth to stifle the cry she knew was coming. Never before had he treated her like this.

Her eyes burned. "Gavin, don't leave. Let's talk now. Please."

He opened the door. "I'll call you tomorrow."

And then he left, shutting the door behind him.

Too numb to move, Marcia simply stood there. When the numbness wore off, pain set in, a pain so harsh that she doubled over and slowly sank to the ground. And then the tears came. Shocked, hurt, confused, she crouched on the floor, her shoulders braced against the door. On the floor, she hugged her knees to her chest and cried for hours until, exhausted, she fell asleep.

When she awoke, she felt somewhat calmer, certain that she must have misunderstood something Gavin had said. Surely he didn't expect her not to go to Vancouver, and surely he would go with her. After all, he was her fiancé. Maybe he'd just been completely shocked by her news and needed time to think about everything.

The following day, when the phone rang, Marcia raced to get it. She just knew it was Gavin and she just knew what he would say.

"Gavin?"

"Yes."

"Oh, Gavin! I've missed you so much."

"I've missed you, too."

Marcia sobbed happily. "Then you'll come over? I really need to see you."

It took Gavin fifteen minutes to arrive. When she greeted him at the door, she hugged him with all the strength she had left in her body, all her love for him. Fighting back tears, she kissed him fiercely, happy to have him back in her arms. She couldn't wait to tell him that she was pregnant.

He spoke before she had the chance. "I'm glad you've decided not to go. Now we can plan our wedding."

Her body grew rigid in his arms. She looked into his eyes. "Gavin, I...didn't decide not to go."

"You didn't? But I thought—I assumed—"

Anguish flooded her. "You don't really expect me to give up this opportunity? You must know I can't do that."

"But I told you yesterday that I would give you time to think this over, and that if you wanted the relationship—"

"Then I'd give up the opportunity of a lifetime?" Her disillusionment was so fierce, it hurt. "I could not possibly agree to that. Just tell me...will you move with me to Vancouver? It will be wonderful if you do." She looked at him imploringly. "Please, Gavin?"

He shook his head. "I thought I made myself clear. Aw, Marcia. I thought you'd make the right choice."

She backed away. He wasn't the man she had fallen madly and passionately in love with. He was an impostor, a cruel stranger, hurting her more than she'd ever thought possible. And she had been a fool to be taken in by him. To believe she could have a life with him. A family.

Nausea hit her, and with it, a spurt of fury.

"You bastard!" she yelled before bursting into tears. "You never loved me. Never!"

He ran his hands over his hair, clearly frustrated. "You're the one who's making the choice."

"You're not giving me a choice!"

She turned away from him, covering her face with both hands. She was dying inside. Yet there was a life growing in her womb. A life she couldn't tell him about. Not while he demonstrated just how little he cared about her by giving her this crazy ultimatum.

She didn't hear Gavin walk out of the living room; she only heard the apartment door squeak. He was leaving her, and he didn't even say goodbye. He simply walked out of her life.

"Marcia, I only want you to be happy." He was standing in the living room again. "And if this is going to make you happy—"

Glaring at him, she yanked the engagement ring off her finger. She marched toward him and stuffed it in his shirt pocket.

Gavin merely stared at the floor, a distant expression on his face.

"Get out!" Marcia cried. "Leave me alone!"

"I'm sorry it had to be this way, Marcia." He turned. Moments later, she heard the apartment door slam shut.

Her life was over, she knew it. Gripping her stomach, thinking of her baby, thinking of all she had just lost, she dropped onto the sofa and cried and cried…

Marcia wiped her eyes as she sat in her cold car, reliving one of the two darkest moments of her life. She had done the right thing this evening. She couldn't believe Gavin's promises, because he had the power to crush her heart once again. She couldn't let him do that.

But making this sudden decision had been difficult. Walking out on Gavin now had been as painful as the first breakup. But the moment he'd mentioned children, she knew. She knew then that they could not have a future together.

Gavin wanted children, and there was no way she could even consider another pregnancy. Her first had ended in disaster, and she had almost died from the despair.

Someday, maybe the memory of her first child would fade, and the pain would subside—but Marcia couldn't see that day coming any time soon.

Not if Gavin was still in her life to constantly remind her.

CHAPTER TWENTY-FIVE

The moment Marcia arrived at Lonita's townhouse, her friend approached her in the vestibule. "Marcia…oh, sweety. What happened? You've been crying."

"I…it's a long story."

Lonita placed a hand on her shoulder. "Gavin called twice. He's worried about you. He wanted to make sure that you got home safely."

"Did he say anything else?"

"Just that you'd left his place over an hour-and-a-half ago. You should call him and let him know you're okay."

"No. I can't."

"Why not?"

"I don't want to talk to him."

"You two had a fight, didn't you?"

Marcia fought back a sob. "It's worse than that. Lonita, it's over."

Lonita embraced her. "I'm so sorry."

Hot tears spilled onto Marcia's cheeks as she accepted her friend's comfort. "So am I."

"Are you sure? He loves you, Marcia. I know that much."

"He was rushing me…moving too fast."

The phone rang. Marcia stiffened.

Lonita asked, "What if it's Gavin?"

"Tell him I'm not here."

"I should at least tell him you're okay."

"Then tell him I'm sleeping. I don't want to talk to him."

Lonita hurried to answer the phone. Marcia followed, staying just close enough to hear the conversation.

"Gavin…yes, she's here. She's sleeping…I'll tell her you called. Bye."

"Thank you," Marcia said when Lonita disconnected.

Arms folded over her chest, Lonita walked toward her. "Do you want to tell me what happened?"

Numbly, Marcia shook her head. Lonita didn't know her secret. How could she tell her now? "I'd like to lie down for a while."

"Okay. I'll be here when you get up, if you want to talk."

Slowly, like an old, tired woman, Marcia dragged herself to bed. Why, if she made the right decision, did she hurt so much? She wanted to sleep…forget…not feel any more…

She was in that room, the frightful room with no windows and no other people.

How did she get here? She couldn't remember.

Instinctively, she clutched her belly. Horror seized her. Where was her baby?

They had taken the baby from her!

She tried to scream, but no sound came out. The harder she tried, the more helpless she felt and the more her head ached.

"Please," she prayed silently. "Bring my baby back to me. Bring him back."

Then she heard him. Faintly at first, but the sound grew louder.

It was her baby! She could hear the soft gurgling sounds a baby makes. Her eyes filled with tears of relief. He was close. She looked around the room but couldn't see him.

Swinging her legs over the side of the bed, she gingerly brought one foot to the floor, then the other.

Now, it sounded as if the baby was under the bed. She dropped to her knees, searching the dark shadows beneath the bed, but her baby wasn't there.

He was outside the door. No longer gurgling happily, but crying.

She ran to the door, but it wouldn't open. She panicked. Her baby was crying right outside the door, and she couldn't get to him.

She pounded the door with her fists, pounded it with her body. But despite her efforts, it didn't open.

And then she didn't hear her baby anymore. She was back on the bed, nurses pinning her down. A physician, syringe in hand, telling her sternly to be calm. Her baby was dead.

She screamed, struggling, fighting off the clutching hands. But as she sat up, she saw that it was not a nurse holding her. It was Lonita, trying to rouse her from the nightmare.

"Marcia...Marcia, you're dreaming."

Dazed, she sat for several moments, inhaling deep breaths to calm her frantic breathing.

"Goodness, you look terrified. You're shivering. Can I get you anything? Water?"

"Yes. Please."

Within minutes, Lonita returned with a tall glass of water. Marcia took the glass from her and drank.

"Thanks."

Lonita sat down beside her. "You kept saying, 'My baby. My baby.'"

"I—I did?" Marcia asked, horrified.

"Yes. Do you remember what you were dreaming about?"

Marcia looked away.

Lonita said, "You know you can tell me. No matter how bad it is."

"I can't."

"One look at you, and I can tell this is eating you up." Lonita placed a reassuring hand on Marcia's shoulder. "It won't help to keep this bottled up. Talk to me. I'm your best friend."

Marcia's mouth felt dry. Could she tell Lonita? She hadn't told anyone.

Lonita said simply, "Trust me."

Four years of trying to be strong, of trying to deal with her secret pain, caught up with Marcia. The burden was finally too great to bear alone. It always had been.

"I don't know where to start."

"The beginning is fine."

Marcia summoned all the courage she had. "You remember why Gavin and I originally broke up?"

"He wanted you to give up your career for him."

"There's more to the story…something I haven't told anyone." Marcia hesitated. "When Gavin gave me that ultimatum, I was pregnant."

"You—pregnant?"

"Yes. And I never told him."

"But he would have—"

"He would have forced me to stay in Toronto and raise his child. Maybe he deserved to know, but I didn't think he loved me. Not after that ultimatum."

Lonita was silent. After a few moments she asked, "What happened to the baby?"

"He…he died."

"Oh, no." Lonita's eyes misted. "Marcia, I'm so sorry. How?"

"He was stillborn. In Vancouver. I gave birth to him, but he was already dead."

Lonita hugged her. "How awful. Oh, Marcia, how did you deal with something like that…alone?"

"I…" She couldn't tell her the worst part. She was too ashamed. "It was very hard."

"It all makes sense now. Rachel's baby shower…why you left. This had to be an incredible burden."

"It was." And to Marcia's surprise, opening up about the pregnancy gave her a modicum of relief. "So, you see, I lost much more than Gavin when we broke up. I lost our child."

"And he still doesn't know?"

Marcia shook her head. "That's why I had to end it. He wants to get married and have children, but I can't do that. Not again."

"Don't you think that if you told him about it the way you've just told me, that he would understand?"

"No. I can't tell him. He would hate me."

"He loves you."

"He'd blame me. For losing his child. He'd say that if I had stayed in Toronto with him, we'd still have our baby."

"You know what I think? I think you're blaming yourself. You think that leaving Gavin caused you to lose your baby, but you can't know that."

Marcia stood. "But you don't know how miserable I was when I left. It must have affected the baby. If I had just stayed here, in Toronto with Gavin, I would have his son, and we would be a family right now."

"You don't know that."

"What kind of person am I? I chose my career over my child." The tears fell, and she couldn't stop them.

Lonita rose and pulled her friend into a hug. "You're one of the best people I know. You can't beat yourself up like this. It's not going to change the past."

"But it's all my fault."

Lonita looked at her. "No. It's not your fault. People lose babies all the time. No one knows why. Only God knows."

"It's not fair. I wanted him. I loved him so much."

"I know. Sweety, I know. Gavin will understand."

"He won't. Not after all this time."

"You just told me, and I understand."

Marcia pulled away.

Lonita changed the subject. "You look exhausted. You need to rest. I've got some sleeping pills."

"No." Marcia's refusal was quick. "I'll be fine. Thanks for listening to me. Thanks for understanding."

"That's what friends are for."

When Lonita was gone, Marcia snuggled under the covers. Maybe her friend was right. Maybe she should tell Gavin. But she couldn't.

CHAPTER TWENTY-SIX

The next morning, Marcia was sipping mint tea when the phone rang. A chill swept over her. She could not answer the phone. Not when it could be Gavin. She let the answering machine pick up.

"Lonita, this is Jackson. I'm trying to reach Marcia."

Marcia picked up the receiver. Despite the fact that she had left Jackson a long time ago, he was still harassing her sister and her friend. "Hello."

"Marcia?" Jackson's voice sounded hopeful.

"Yes, Jackson. It's me. And I have only one thing to say to you. You've been hounding Andrea and Lonita, and it's got to stop."

"I only want to see you."

"I don't want to see you."

Jackson paused, then said, "All right, I'll make you a deal. I promise that if you see me one last time, I'll stop bothering your sister. And Lonita."

Marcia opened her mouth to protest, but Jackson was already speaking again.

"I want to apologize in person, Marcia. I want to see you, even if it is for one last time."

She frowned. She didn't owe him anything, but she did owe something to her sister and Lonita.

"If that's what it takes to stop you from pestering them, then I'll agree to one last meeting."

Smiling widely, Jackson rose when Marcia approached the small corner table where he was waiting for her.

Marcia was tense. "What's this all about, Jackson?"

"It's good to see you." He moved to hug her, but she slipped into a seat.

"I don't have a lot of time."

"Then I'll get to the point." Sitting, he reached across the table and took her hand. "I want to apologize, Marcia."

"Very well, apology accepted." Freeing her hand, she pushed her chair back, fully intending to leave.

But Jackson said, "Please stay. I also want to explain. Won't you…won't you please let me?"

Marcia knew she should leave, but for some reason, she felt sorry for Jackson. Maybe he needed to get the guilt off his chest once and for all.

"It doesn't matter anymore, Jackson. But if it makes you feel better, I'll listen."

"Marcia, I don't know what was going on in my mind when I got involved with Sandy. She's one of the writers for the show. I don't know. I think that somewhere inside me I figured if I didn't sleep with her she'd write me out of the script."

"For goodness' sake, Jackson! Will you at least be honest? You and I both know that if the director and producer like you, as well as the television audience, there's no way you'll be written out of the show."

He sighed wearily. "Okay. You're right. The point is, I just wasn't thinking. I'd been going to a lot of the cast parties, drinking a lot—things I didn't used to do. You know that."

"Yes, I do know. And when I tried to tell you about it, you got defensive."

"I'm sorry about that, Marcia. You don't know how much. I really need you in my life—that's what I've realized. I can't live without you."

"You should have thought about that before."

The waiter appeared and took their order, then disappeared quickly.

Jackson fiddled with the salt shaker. "You probably don't know this, but things aren't going well on the show."

Marcia's eyes widened in surprise. "Why not?"

"Because I've screwed up. I've let this whole star thing get to my head."

"I'm glad you've finally realized that. But you can change. You're a good actor. Just don't let your ego take over."

"That's why I need you, Marcia." He reached for her hand again, clasping it as if it was a life preserver. "When I was with you, I was a different person. I was happier…I was real. I've lost touch with that side of myself, and I need you in my life again."

Bereft of words, Marcia glanced down at the table. Jackson wanted her back. Just as Gavin had wanted her back.

Firmly, she freed her hand. "Jackson, I…we can't."

"Because of Gavin?" His tone was irritated.

The waiter reappeared with their drinks, saving Marcia from having to answer. She certainly didn't want to talk to Jackson about Gavin.

When the waiter left the table, Jackson said, "I'm right, aren't I?"

"Gavin has nothing to do with this."

"Give me another chance, Marcia. I love you."

"You don't know what love is. And I don't want to get involved with you again."

"I want to marry you, Marcia."

Her breath caught. "You must be crazy."

Jackson reached into his jacket pocket. He withdrew a small, pink velvet box and slid it across the table. "Open it."

Marcia swallowed, her throat suddenly dry and tight. There was no doubt what was in the box. If Jackson had proposed months ago, had presented her with a velvet ring box when things were good…

She shook her head. "It's too late, Jackson."

"It's never too late." His eyes dark and compelling, he pressed the box into her hand, closing her fingers around it. "Open it, Marcia."

Curiosity had always been her besetting sin. Without a second thought, she raised the pink velvet lid...and could only stare, speechless, at the exquisite, very large marquise-cut diamond. It was flawless and must have cost Jackson a fortune.

"Do you like it?" Jackson's voice held a note of smugness. He knew she liked what she saw. What could be more beautiful?

Only the modest pear-shaped diamond Gavin had given her.

The wayward thought startled her, and the prick of tears even more. She blinked, forcing her attention back to Jackson.

"Marry me, Marcia," he said urgently. "I love you."

She closed the box. "I'm sorry, Jackson. Our relationship ended when I found out that you were seeing other women. Even if I can forgive you, it's not something I can forget."

He seemed surprised. "But I need you, Marcia! Nothing is going right without you."

"Again, I'm sorry. But I, too, have needs."

Even if she wasn't quite sure what they were.

"Goodbye, Jackson. Good luck."

Squarely setting the ring box on the place mat in front of him, she rose and left.

"I don't believe it." Marcia's mother sat on the sofa beside her. "He proposed?"

"No one was more surprise than I. I only agreed to meet him because he'd been badgering Andrea and Lonita. I didn't expect a proposal."

"He sounds desperate."

"Yeah. Desperate to keep his ego intact. I don't get it. Did he really think I would take that ring? That I would simply forget about what he did to me?"

"No doubt, he was hoping."

"Why do men do that? Insist on pressuring women, expect too much, make assumptions, want everything to go the way they want it to all the time…?"

"Why do I think you're no longer talking about Jackson?"

The back of Marcia's neck prickled and she looked away from her mother's probing gaze. "Of course I am."

"I know you and Gavin are…having problems."

Marcia's shoulders slumped. "That's an understatement. Mom, we broke up."

"I thought you two were working things out. What happened?"

"It's a long story—"

"I've got the time."

Marcia brought one foot up onto the sofa. "There were too many unresolved issues."

"Like?"

"Like things we wouldn't be able to work out."

Her mother eyed her dubiously. "Did you talk to him about them? I know you like to keep things to yourself sometimes."

"The bottom line is, I don't want to get hurt again."

"You didn't answer me."

"It wouldn't have mattered, Mom. The issues were too big. Sure, things were going fine for a while, but what would happen down the road when these issues came back to haunt me...us? I can't deal with that kind of hurt again, Mom. I can't."

"You don't seem to be dealing with it too well now."

"I'll get over it."

Concern clouded Mrs. Robertson's face. "Look at you. You've got dark circles under your eyes. And you've definitely lost weight. Are you even eating, sleeping?"

"I've been busy, working. Thank goodness."

"So you're just going to lose yourself in your work and forget about your happiness?"

Marcia picked at imaginary lint on her jeans. "If that's what it takes."

"He's called here, you know."

Marcia's heart fluttered. "He has?" Was that how her mother had found out about their problems? "What did he say?"

"He called to say hi, and that he would keep in touch even though you weren't dating anymore. He also wanted to know how you were doing."

Every time she learned that Gavin had called for her, she felt a tremendous amount of guilt. She remembered the look on his face the night she ended their relationship, that sad, desolate look. It would be so much easier if he just stopped calling her, if he got on with his life.

"Do you love him?"

Love. She hadn't wanted to think about that emotion. It was too dangerous. "We were getting close again..."

"It was more than that. I saw you two together. You were never that happy, not even with Jackson."

"How can I know what love is, Mom? I haven't had a successful relationship."

"You do. Sweetheart, you do. It's staring you right in the face. Why do you think it hurts so much if you're not in love with him?"

Her mother was right. So right. She had been denying her feelings, trying to guard her heart. But she couldn't deny the truth any longer. She was in love with Gavin. She always had been.

"I do love him, Mom. But I'm afraid. He hurt me too much the first time."

"You cannot live your life in fear. Life is too short for that."

Marcia ran a hand over her face. "I'm confused. I'm not sure what I want."

"What does your heart say?"

"That…I miss him." That she should stop running. That she was afraid his opinion of her would change after he learned her darkest secrets.

"Then call him, Marcia. Work it out."

CHAPTER TWENTY-SEVEN

Gavin flipped through the manila folder containing his notes and evaluations of Jessica Sanders-Harmon, as well of some of her sample works. There were selected stories, artwork, math assignments, and work from other areas of the curriculum. She was one of the brighter students in his class, and he should be looking forward to the first parent-teacher interview with her father.

Instead, he was restless and could not wait to go home. All he could think about was Marcia, and how he could reach her.

Pushing back his chair, he rose. She wouldn't take his calls, wouldn't let him visit her at Lonita's and explain. How was he going to convince her that they could build a life together?

He looked at his watch. It was eleven-thirty-three and Michael Harmon, Jessica's father, was due to arrive at any moment. Gavin had met the girl's mother before, but as the parents were divorced, he had yet to meet the father. From what he understood, Ms. Sanders had sole custody of her daughter, but Jessica spent weekends with her father. Because of their custody arrangement, even this meeting with Mr. Harmon had to be approved by Ms. Sanders.

Thankfully, this was his last interview before lunch. Crossing the room, Gavin went to the window and looked outside. The wind blew, shaking the barren trees. The sky was gray. It looked like it might snow.

He heard footsteps and turned toward the classroom door, where a dark-haired man in his late thirties or early forties stood, hesitating.

Extending a hand, Gavin approached him. "Mr. Harmon, I presume? Come in, please. I'm Gavin Williams."

"I'm glad to meet you at last, Mr. Williams. My daughter goes on and on about you."

"She's a pleasure to have in my class." Gavin led Michael Harmon to a table equipped with two chairs and invited him to have a seat while they examined samples of Jessica's work and Gavin shared his observations of her progress. They discussed Jessica's actual report card for a few minutes, then Gavin asked, "Is there anything you want to ask me?"

Michael Harmon smiled. "What can I say? 'Exceeds expectations' in every category is the best a father can hope for. I'm very pleased."

"So am I. Jessica is a diligent and thorough worker. She works well on her own and in a group. And she's always eager to help others. Overall, I think she's a wonderful little girl, and I'm very pleased with her progress."

"I always worry about her. She took the divorce very hard. I understand she's doing well academically, but how is she emotionally? Any problems that you've noticed?"

"Nothing, really. Sometimes she seems a bit sad, but that's normal. Mostly she's happy, friendly. Outgoing."

"Like her mother. You know she's a screenwriter?"

"Yes. Jessica keeps me informed of the shows her mother is working on. She wants to be a writer, like her mother, she says." Gavin leaned back in his chair. "I don't believe she's mentioned what you do. If she has, I've forgotten."

"I'm a talent agent."

"So the entertainment business runs in the family."

"You could say that."

"I used to date an actress once," Gavin said, unable to keep his thoughts off of Marcia. "Actually, we were engaged."

"A Toronto actress?"

Gavin nodded. "She did a lot of work. Still does."

"What's her name? The Toronto entertainment community is small. Maybe I know her."

"Marcia Robertson."

"For goodness' sake!" Mr. Harmon exclaimed. "I represent her!"

"Really?"

"Yeah. I've represented her for—" He stopped and calculated the years in his mind. "Six years. Almost seven."

"That's when I used to date her. What's your agency name?"

"Michael Harmon Management."

Gavin shrugged. "That doesn't sound familiar."

"I should have recognized your name. Gavin Williams...of course. Marcia was crazy about you. It's true what they say. It's definitely a small world. I'm glad to finally meet you."

"Likewise."

"It's a shame what happened. It must have been really hard on you both."

Gavin nodded tersely. "It was."

"To lose a baby—it's understandable why you two broke up. Not many relationships survive that kind of stress."

Too stunned to speak, Gavin merely stared. Baby? Marcia had been pregnant?

Harmon patted Gavin on the shoulder. "But you're the one who went through it. You certainly don't need me to tell you how stressful losing a child is."

Gavin finally found his voice. "What did you say? Marcia was pregnant?"

Michael Harmon stared at him, horrified by his own presumptuous carelessness."You didn't know?"

"She was pregnant with my child?"

Harmon hesitated. "I—look, if Marcia didn't tell you any of this, then it's not my place."

"You've said too much to back off now." To his surprise, Gavin sounded very calm. But his heart was pounding. His palms were sweating. Marcia could not have been pregnant and kept something like that from him. "Tell me the rest."

"I'm sorry I can't help you. You'll have to speak with Marcia." Michael Harmon pushed his chair back and stood. "Thanks for filling me in on Jessica's progress. Goodbye, Mr. Williams."

Left alone, Gavin stayed at the conference table. He couldn't have been more winded if he had been pounded in the gut with a sledge hammer.

A baby.

He looked at his shaking hands. Marcia had been pregnant with his baby. But their child had died.

His stomach clenched. Perhaps Michael Harmon had made a mistake. But, after briefly considering the possibility, Gavin dismissed it. He slumped in the chair, feeling as wiped out as he had when he learned of his brother's death. And yet his emotions were different this time, more complicated because he had not known that he was a father.

Had not known.

Adrenaline surged through his blood, warming him, fueling anger. Why on earth hadn't Marcia told him? How could she keep something like this from him? Even though they had broken up, he had a right to know. She should have told him that she was pregnant and what had happened to their child.

His child!

He must see her. Today.

When the last parent-teacher interview was over, Gavin rushed to the staff room.

He dialed Lonita's phone number. After two rings, the answering machine picked up. If Marcia was there, she was undoubtedly screening the calls. Avoiding him. And now he knew why.

A phone call would not do. Marcia would only run again if she knew he was coming. Hanging up the phone, he grabbed his leather jacket.

Snow flurries whirled in the sky, leaving the ground moist as they touched its surface. Gavin cursed under his breath. He didn't want anything hindering his ability to get to Marcia as quickly as possible.

When he arrived at Lonita's, his stomach knotted. Even though he was desperate to see her, it would be hard to look at her, to look into the eyes of the woman he had trusted, the woman who had betrayed that trust.

He pounded on the door. Pounded again. Nobody answered. Hurrying back to his car, Gavin wondered where Marcia could be. If she wasn't home, maybe she was working. And if she was working, her agent would know where she was.

Back in his car, he used his cell phone to call directory assistance. He got Michael Harmon's office number from the operator and, a few moments later, had the man on the phone.

"Harmon, this is Gavin Williams. I need to locate Marcia. Today. Is she on a set?"

"Sorry, I don't give out information on my clients."

"You already did. Come on, Harmon! This is important."

"I don't want to get involved."

"You already are." Gavin hesitated. "This has been a shock to me. You know that. And now I need to reach Marcia. See her in person. She won't take my calls."

Michael Harmon was silent.

Gavin pressed. "You're a father. I'm sure you can appreciate that I have the right to know about my child. Marcia told you, but she didn't tell me. And I was the baby's father!"

"I'm her agent. I knew about the pregnancy only because of the show."

"I should have known. Please. I need to know where she is. I need to talk to her."

Silence. Gavin gritted his teeth.

"All right. But I can't guarantee she's still there. She started work early this morning, and she could very well be wrapped right now."

"I'll take my chances."

"The address is twenty-two thirty-three Lakeshore Boulevard West. Studio D. Look, I know you're angry, but please—"

"Thanks." Gavin flipped his cell phone shut.

The location wasn't too far, but traffic was a nightmare at this time of day, especially with snow flurries. What should have taken him twenty minutes took forty-five minutes instead, and all the while he prayed that he wouldn't be too late. He had to see her. Had to hear from her why she had never told him about the baby.

He found the studio, and in his haste, swerved into the entrance, cutting off another driver. A horn blared. Through his rearview mirror, he could see hands flailing from the car he cut off. He didn't have time to worry about that. He needed to get to Marcia.

He squeezed into a parking spot and was out of the car almost before he had cut the engine. The studio was a large warehouse with several doors. He walked around until he saw the sign "Studio D." Outside stood a man wearing a walkie-talkie headset like receptionists wore. Gavin approached him.

"Excuse me. I'm wondering if Marcia Robertson is still here."

"And she would be…?"

"An actress. I'm supposed to pick her up."

"You'll have to check with an A.D." The man opened the door. "Go straight ahead. You'll find one inside."

"Thanks."

Inside, Gavin was surrounded by darkness, but he could see a well-lit area not too far off. He started walking toward the lights, his footsteps loud on the concrete floor. Before long, a short, harried-looking man intercepted him.

"Can I help you?"

Gavin tried to look authoritative. "I'm looking for Marcia Robertson."

"She's filming right now, but you can wait, I suppose."

Gavin nodded. He'd found her. If need be, he'd wait all night.

"Rolling! Quiet please!" someone shouted from out of nowhere, and red lights above the doors began flashing. The short, harried-looking man motioned for Gavin to follow him quietly.

"Speed," someone else said.

"Background action!"

"And action!"

Gavin crept closer to the brightly lit set until he came to an area where several men and women had congregated around a small color monitor that displayed the scene as it was being filmed. For a moment, he watched the actors on the monitor, then glanced at the actual set. He had never been on a film set before and, despite his impatience to confront Marcia, found himself caught up in the proceedings. In fact, he was fascinated.

The set was constructed to look like an old police station. There were desks, bulletin boards, fake windows with artificial light flowing through them, doors leading to offices, and even a coffee machine. He always thought when he watched television that scenes were actually filmed in whatever the location appeared to be. But here, there was no doubt that this mock police station was just that—artificial. The station's three walls were propped up by studs. Occupying the space where the fourth wall would have been were the camera and the crew. It was amazing.

So far, he hadn't see Marcia. Several people dressed in police uniforms had walked across the set at various times. Extras, Gavin surmised. Two men in dark suits, one older and one middle-aged, spoke their lines in the middle of the room.

Then Marcia entered, escorted by a uniformed officer. Gavin's interest piqued and he strained to hear what they were saying.

"Sergeant Trotsky," the officer said, "this is Mrs. Whitfield."

The older of the dark-suited men shook hands with Marcia, dressed in a simple blue dress with a gray sweater. "I'm glad you agreed to come in, Mrs. Whitfield."

Marcia or, rather, Mrs. Whitfield, clasped her hands nervously. "I don't know how I can help you." Her voice held a note of apprehension. "I already explained everything to the officer."

The sergeant nodded. "There's a different matter that I think you can assist us in." He looked at the uniformed police officer. "That'll be all for now, Lesarge."

The officer walked away, and when he was out of the camera's range, propped himself against a desk.

"Please come with me," the sergeant said to Marcia.

She gave him a quick, frightened look, then followed him into an office.

"Cut!" That came from the man who was sitting directly in front of the small monitor. Gavin assumed he was the director. "That was great. I want to do one more before we move in for close-ups."

From what little he saw of the scene, Gavin was impressed. He didn't know what role Marcia was playing, but she had convinced him that the Mrs. Whitfield character was apprehensive.

He thought of the reason he was here, and couldn't help but feel guilty for the way he had ignored her aspirations before. Maybe if he had taken the time to get to know what her job was like, and why she loved it so much, he would not have given her that ultimatum. Maybe. But perhaps, he had needed the years overseas and his mother's illness to reach maturity.

But no matter what, Marcia should have told him she was carrying their child.

He watched them do the scene not once but four more times before he decided to slip out and wait in the parking lot. He didn't want Marcia to see him in the studio. That might prove an unwelcome distraction for her.

He waited in the car for two hours before he finally saw people spilling out of the building, getting into cars, and driving away. It was dark now, but the parking lot was well lit. He had no trouble spotting Marcia.

Slowly, he got out of the car. Now that the moment of confrontation had come, he was hesitant, unsure of himself. Where was the anger that had brought him here? All he felt was a deep sadness.

"I'll see you tomorrow," he heard her say to a companion. She was walking straight toward him, but she was rummaging through her purse and didn't notice him.

He stepped in front of her, blocking her path. "Marcia."

She looked up, startled. The purse slipped from her hands.

He picked it up. How tired she looked. "I'm sorry if I scared you."

"No…yes, I suppose you did. You surprised me." She accepted her purse with shaking hands.

He watched her. Surprise would not make her look as miserable as she did. It was almost as if she knew why he wanted to speak to her.

"Marcia, did Harmon warn you that I was coming to see you?"

"My agent?" Confusion crossed her face. "No. And I can't…I can't speak to you now. I'm exhausted."

He caught her arm as she turned away. "Not this time, Marcia. You can't always run away from explanations. Tell me about the baby. Our baby."

"Oh, God!" In the parking lights' glare, the stricken look in her eyes was unmistakable. "How…?"

"That doesn't matter. The point is that I do know. At last." He hesitated. "Why, Marcia? Why didn't you tell me?"

"You never gave me the chance!"

"You have the chance right now."

"I-I can't! Not now."

"I have a right to know."

"I need time, Gavin!"

"Time?" He suddenly wanted to shake her. Or drag her off and hold her captive until they'd made another baby. The violence of his emotions shook him. Dropping her arm, he stepped back, putting a safe distance between them. "You've had more than four years. How much longer do you need?"

"Until it doesn't hurt anymore!" she cried. "Until I can believe you won't judge me!"

She fled to her car as if certain that he would stop her if he caught her. But he stood, immobilized and helpless in the face of her pain.

CHAPTER TWENTY-EIGHT

Marcia drove off as if pursued.

Why did Gavin have to catch her by surprise? She had been trying for weeks to gather the courage to see him, to tell him everything. She would have done it soon, but then to be so suddenly confronted by him!

Stomach churning, emotions whirling, she ran up the stairs of Lonita's home. The door opened as she reached for the handle.

"Marcia!" Andrea exclaimed. Lonita stood behind her.

"Great, you're home. We were heading out to The Palace. Come with us."

Marcia walked past them, kicking off her shoes as she stepped inside. "Not tonight, sis. I'm pretty tired."

Lonita approached her. "Come on. It's been a long time since you went dancing with us."

"Yeah," Andrea agreed. "You've been working so much lately. You deserve a break."

"Another time." With shaking hands, Marcia removed her jacket and hung it in the closet.

"You're sure?" Andrea asked. "We don't mind waiting, do we, Lonita?"

Lonita shook her head. "Of course not."

"Thanks." Marcia forced a smile. "Maybe tomorrow."

Andrea and Lonita said their goodbyes and left. After watching their car disappear from the driveway, Marcia collapsed on her bed in the spare room.

Not even a night of dancing would make her forget the look in Gavin's eyes, that devastated, grief-stricken look. It haunted her in the hours that followed. In his eyes she had seen a grief that equaled her own when she had lost the baby.

"I have a right to know." The very quietness of his tone had reproached her.

Guilt overwhelmed her, made her feel drained, ashamed. His disapproval, his blame was what she had feared all along. And now, how could he not hate her, now that he knew the truth? She should have been the one to tell him; instead, he had heard it from a stranger. She should have stayed with him this evening, should have tried to explain. Instead, she had run. As she had in the past.

Marcia clung to her pillow in the darkened bedroom and suddenly felt very alone. She couldn't continue like this, a weak shell of a woman, always running, always trying to hide from pain. It was no way to live.

She wanted to be with Gavin. Wanted to make him understand. Wanted to know that he didn't hate her. She wanted to tell him how wrong she was to have kept the truth from him. But she was afraid. Afraid that he would reject her.

And if she did not tell him the truth, she would always be miserable. Brokenhearted. Alone. She had loved him once, and lost him. Her soul mate. She had given him up without a fight, without telling him about the baby. Maybe if she had stood her ground, told him about the baby, made him understand her love for her career, they could have worked things out. But she had run away.

Incredibly, she had been given a second chance at happiness when Gavin reappeared in her life. And she had blown it by running away once again.

Or had she?

Abruptly, Marcia sat up. She couldn't possibly feel more alone, more desolate than she did right now. So what did she have to lose by telling Gavin the truth? She could not lose his love since she did not have it now. She could not lose his respect since she did not have it now. And if she gained nothing else, at least she would regain her dignity.

Drawing on a reserve of strength she didn't know she possessed, she snatched her purse and coat and dashed out to her car. It was time to confront her fears, her demons. To face the truth.

To fight for her happiness. For her love. Her soul mate.

Gavin would think she was crazy. He would think she was absolutely out of her mind. And Marcia couldn't blame him. It was shortly after midnight, and all reason told her that she should not be here on his doorstep, but she was. She rang the doorbell. And rang it again.

Several minutes later, the porch light flickered to life. The door jerked open.

"For goodness' sake—" Heavy-lidded and grumpy, Gavin stopped mid-sentence when he saw Marcia.

"Gavin." His name tumbled from her lips softly, sounding more like a plea than anything else. The sight of him, dressed only in blue cotton pajama pants, his hard chest and strong arms naked and exposed, did not go unnoticed by her. He was a beautiful creature. And she loved him.

"It's late, Marcia."

He seemed wary, distant, and Marcia's stomach twisted into a knot of doubt. But there would be no more running away.

She squared her shoulders. "You were right, Gavin. I owe you an explanation."

"It's cold. Come in."

Until now, she hadn't realized that she was shivering and that her toes in flimsy high-heeled shoes were icy cold. Stepping onto the doormat, she stomped her feet, as much to warm them as to shake off specks of snow clinging to her shoes.

Without speaking, Gavin took her coat and hung it on a rack. His expression was guarded, and Marcia couldn't tell what he was thinking. No matter, she had to go through with this. She had to make him understand.

He started for the living room. Determined not to be discouraged by his distant manner, she followed, watching the muscles in his back move gracefully beneath the sleek brown skin.

"Trust me," he had once said. But she hadn't. Now she was about to bare her soul. If he didn't forgive her, it would be her own fault. But at least he would know the truth.

"Go ahead, sit down."

She eased onto the sofa, folding her hands in her lap. He remained standing.

She looked up at him. "I'm sorry to come here so late. It's just that...I needed to see you. Tonight."

Gavin steeled his jaw.

"I'm here to tell you the truth. About the baby...our baby."

Finally, a flicker of emotion crossed his face, but Marcia couldn't tell what it was. Sadness, perhaps. Or anger.

"It's hard to believe," he said. "We made a baby, and you didn't tell me. I never thought you'd keep something like that from me."

"I'm sorry." She hugged her arms to her body. "I never meant to hurt you, I swear. I was just so hurt myself."

"So hurt that you couldn't talk to me?"

"I was scared. When I told you I'd landed that part in Vancouver, and you refused to move there with me..."

"Yes? Go on."

"That was only half the good news I planned to tell you that day. I was also going to tell you that I was pregnant. But then you delivered your ultimatum."

Frowning, he crossed his arms. "You knew then, before you went to Vancouver?"

"I was devastated when you forced me to choose between you and my career. I was in shock. I didn't think you loved me."

"If I had known you were pregnant—"

"Then what?" She stared into Gavin's eyes, so dark, so intense. "You would have changed your mind and come with me?"

His gaze fell.

She said, "Maybe you would have, but you were so adamant I was sure you would force me to stay in Toronto—to give up the best career opportunity of my life."

"You still should have told me."

"I realize that. But I was hurt. I couldn't bear to tell you when I thought you didn't really love me."

"You didn't trust me." He sounded accusing. "You didn't trust my love for you."

"How could I, when I found out your love had conditions? I could have dealt with anything...anything but that."

Abruptly, he turned and started to pace. But after a few steps he faced her again.

"Marcia, I never told you the real reason why I didn't want you to take that part."

"Yes, you did. You said you couldn't leave your family. You said I should get a proper job, that the life of an actress wasn't stable enough to raise a family."

"Those weren't my reasons." His voice was low. "I, too, was afraid. Afraid that I would lose you to your career. The way I lost my father to his music."

His honesty, his vulnerability, touched her heart. He, too, was bearing his soul. Until now, all he had told her was how much he regretted giving her that ultimatum, but not why he had. And she needed to know.

"He loved us," Gavin continued. "But the more he wanted to follow his dream, the more we got in the way. And then he simply left. Right after Angela was born. He walked out and never looked back."

"I'm sorry." She rose, wanting to close at least the physical distance between them, even if she couldn't change their emotional separation.

He had never told her about his father before, only that his parents divorced when he was very young. And that they had received no support from his father, hadn't even been able to contact him when Marcus died. Looking at Gavin now, Marcia realized the depth of his pain.

He said, "You were the best thing that ever happened to me. I couldn't bear the thought of losing you. Not after losing my father, my brother. That was why I forced you to make a choice. But if I'd known you were pregnant—Marcia, what happened to the baby? How did it die?"

CHAPTER TWENTY-NINE

The suddenness of the question was like a blow. Marcia reeled, tears pricking her eyes.

"Marcia?" Gavin took a step toward her but did not touch her. "Can you talk about the baby?"

Yes, she could. It was why she had rushed across town in the middle of the night.

She took a deep breath. "I lost it."

"You had a miscarriage?"

"He...was stillborn."

Gavin's mouth twisted painfully. "He?"

"Yes. It was a little boy."

"And he was stillborn?"

"Yes."

He spoke slowly, with an effort. "You should have called me. Told me. I should have been there for you."

"I couldn't tell anyone."

"I was his father."

"But you were no longer in my life. I felt alone...so alone. I didn't think I had anyone to turn to. I'd lost you. I'd lost my job on the show. Then I lost my...son."

She couldn't control the tears anymore. She couldn't control the sobs. She needed to mourn one last time.

With Gavin.

She didn't know who moved first, but the distance between them closed, and she was in his arms. He held her tightly, silently, while she cried. And she clung to him, clung to the safety of his solid body, the warmth of his embrace.

"I should have been there for you," he whispered into her hair.

Feeling as if a great burden had been lifted off her shoulders, Marcia sniffled and wiped her eyes.

"Let me get you a tissue."

He released her, disappearing into the kitchen. Moments later he returned. Grateful, she pulled a few tissues from the box and blew her nose.

Taking her hand, Gavin drew her onto the sofa. "You said you lost your job on the show. What happened?"

"I got fired."

"Why?"

"I turned down the director's sexual advances." It was easier and easier to talk about the past. "I guess I hurt his ego. After that, things were really tense. And then, when I started to show—well that was his perfect excuse to get rid of me."

"He didn't want you to have the baby?"

Marcia shrugged. "I don't know. I don't care. If I hadn't been pregnant, the director would have found another reason to get rid of me. Either that, or I would have left."

"I'm sorry. I wish I had known."

The warm look in his eyes, the concern, shook Marcia. Her tale wasn't finished. She needed to go on, to tell him the worst part of all.

"What you don't know, Gavin, what nobody knows…is what happened to me after I lost our son."

"What happened, Marcia? Will you tell me now?"

She nodded. She wouldn't keep it from him anymore. Keeping this secret had prevented her from truly healing.

"I was devastated when I lost our son. I blamed myself, my selfishness for wanting the job more than a secure family life for the baby. If I had stayed in Toronto with you—"

Again, she had to battle tears. "The doctors said it wasn't my fault, that these things sometimes happen. But I truly believed that because I was so unhappy without you, the baby knew…he felt he wasn't wanted."

Gavin gently wiped the fresh tears. "I hope you don't still believe that."

"Sometimes I do. You don't know what it's like, carrying a baby inside you for nine months, only to have it…die. I couldn't help but blame myself, Gavin. I felt I was being punished…for leaving you, for not telling you I was pregnant."

"Marcia, don't." He cradled her face in his hands. "I'm the one to blame here."

She searched his eyes and felt strengthened. "No, Gavin. Don't assume a burden you needn't carry. Just let me tell you the rest. You see, I…couldn't handle it. The guilt. The depression. I—" She swallowed hard. "I had a nervous breakdown."

He turned ashen.

"I just couldn't function, Gavin." She spoke faster, the words tumbling over each other. "I was hospitalized. For months. I couldn't handle life. I didn't want to die but was afraid to live. I was tormented. Felt all alone…"

"You shouldn't have been alone, Marcia." His voice was husky, ripe with emotion. He wrapped his arms around her. "I should have been there for you."

"I was too ashamed to face anybody. My family, friends, you. Only my agent knew about the baby, and that I was taking time off to cope with my loss. Not even he knows about the breakdown. That was the darkest point of my life, and I didn't want anyone—you—to think ill of me."

"I could never think ill of you."

"But I couldn't be sure of that. That's why I didn't tell you."

He searched her face. "So why are you telling me now?"

"Because you deserve the truth. Because this is the only way I can find peace. That night when you proposed, when you mentioned children, everything—all the painful memories—came rushing back. I got scared. Scared that history would repeat itself. And I couldn't bear that. Not again."

Gavin held her tightly. "I'm sorry, Marcia. So sorry for what I put you through. If I had gone with you, if I'd had the strength to trust your love for me—"

"It's not your fault." Marcia pulled back and lovingly caressed Gavin's jaw. "Please, don't blame yourself. I only told you this to make you understand."

"I do understand. But I can't forget what you had to go through. I was such a fool!"

"Gavin, this is a time for forgiveness. We need to forgive each other...ourselves." Her voice was gentle. "I forgive you, Gavin."

He looked at her for a long time, then nodded. "You're right. It's the only way. So, listen to me, Marcia. I forgive you. And God knows, I still love you. I want you back in my life. Please tell me we have a chance."

Marcia gazed into his eyes, the eyes of the man who loved her—unconditionally. There were no more doubts. There were no secrets between them, nothing to keep them apart.

"I love you, Gavin. I'll only ever love you."

Tightening his hold, he asked, "Marry me?"

She did not hesitate. "Gavin Williams, I would be honored to be your wife."

"I want you to know, you're all I need. If you feel that having children is something you can't deal with, that's okay. You alone make my life complete."

For a moment, she could only stare at him. Gavin had always wanted children, but he was willing to give up that dream for her. She felt humbled and light-headed. And blissfully happy. How blessed she was to have the love of such a wonderful, caring, selfless man.

"What did I ever do to deserve you?" Tenderly, she placed a palm against his face. "You've given so much. That's why I want to give to you. Gavin, I do want children. Lots of them. As long as they are yours."

A lone tear slid down Gavin's cheek and caught against her hand as he gazed at her with such warmth, such happiness, such love...

"I love you," he said, then planted a soft, sensual kiss on her lips.

A joy she had never known consumed her. Caught in his embrace, she succumbed to the kiss, giving and receiving, loving and being loved.

"Make love to me," she whispered against his mouth.

He scooped her into his arms and carried her upstairs to the bedroom, where he laid her on the bed. Their gazes locked and held as he stretched out beside her. Words were not necessary. The look in their eyes, every touch and caress, told of the love in their hearts, in their souls. Their lovemaking was a promise, commitment. They had no idea that this was the night they would create a life together, the greatest symbol of their love.

EPILOGUE

Exhausted, Marcia leaned against the propped up backrest of the hospital bed. Beads of sweat rolled down her face; her breathing was labored. But the physical discomfort did not matter to her. She was deliriously happy.

She could hear her baby crying, and that was music to her ears. Barely able to contain her exhilaration and impatience as the hospital staff wrapped her baby in a blanket, she held Gavin's hand tightly.

A nurse approached them with the small bundle, a warm smile brightening her face. "He's gorgeous, Mrs. Williams."

Gavin's smile was luminous as the nurse placed the baby in Marcia's arms. He leaned toward his wife and child. "He is perfect. Beautiful."

His gaze met Marcia's. "And so are you, my love. Thank you." He kissed her tenderly. "Thank you for my son."

"Thank you," she whispered.

She looked down at the child in her arms. Marcus Anthony Williams. He was indeed perfect. His skin was a pale brown; his eyes were alert; his head was full of dark, curly hair. And his nose—it was just like the proud father's.

Her heart filled with love. And the bittersweet memory of another baby she had held long ago. An ominously still baby.

But the child in her arms now was warm and alive, amazingly strong legs kicking inside the blanket. Gently, she touched his face, the tiny hands. The kicking stopped as Marcus Anthony stared intently at her. Suddenly, he smiled.

A faint smile, but one that filled Marcia's heart with indescribable bliss.

Excited, she darted a look at Gavin. "Did you see that? He smiled at me!"

"Why wouldn't he?" Perched on the edge of her bed, Gavin stroked her dampened hair. "He's got you for a mother. He knows what a lucky guy he is."

Marcia chuckled delightedly as she looked from her son to her husband. "I'm the lucky one."

She sat up straighter, her child in one arm, the other wrapped around her husband. The two most important loves of her life. They were her world. Her happiness. Her present and future, here in her arms.

Her family. Her dreams come true.

At last.

2008 Reprint Mass Market Titles

January

Cautious Heart
Cheris F. Hodges
ISBN-13: 978-1-58571-301-1
ISBN-10: 1-58571-301-5
$6.99

Suddenly You
Crystal Hubbard
ISBN-13: 978-1-58571-302-8
ISBN-10: 1-58571-302-3
$6.99

February

Passion
T. T. Henderson
ISBN-13: 978-1-58571-303-5
ISBN-10: 1-58571-303-1
$6.99

Whispers in the Sand
LaFlorya Gauthier
ISBN-13: 978-1-58571-304-2
ISBN-10: 1-58571-304-x
$6.99

March

Life Is Never As It Seems
J. J. Michael
ISBN-13: 978-1-58571-305-9
ISBN-10: 1-58571-305-8
$6.99

Beyond the Rapture
Beverly Clark
ISBN-13: 978-1-58571-306-6
ISBN-10: 1-58571-306-6
$6.99

April

A Heart's Awakening
Veronica Parker
ISBN-13: 978-1-58571-307-3
ISBN-10: 1-58571-307-4
$6.99

Breeze
Robin Lynette Hampton
ISBN-13: 978-1-58571-308-0
ISBN-10: 1-58571-308-2
$6.99

May

I'll Be Your Shelter
Giselle Carmichael
ISBN-13: 978-1-58571-309-7
ISBN-10: 1-58571-309-0
$6.99

Careless Whispers
Rochelle Alers
ISBN-13: 978-1-58571-310-3
ISBN-10: 1-58571-310-4
$6.99

June

Sin
Crystal Rhodes
ISBN-13: 978-1-58571-311-0
ISBN-10: 1-58571-311-2
$6.99

Dark Storm Rising
Chinelu Moore
ISBN-13: 978-1-58571-312-7
ISBN-10: 1-58571-312-0
$6.99

2008 Reprint Mass Market Titles (continued)

July

Object of His Desire
A.C. Arthur
ISBN-13: 978-1-58571-313-4
ISBN-10: 1-58571-313-9
$6.99

Angel's Paradise
Janice Angelique
ISBN-13: 978-1-58571-314-1
ISBN-10: 1-58571-314-7
$6.99

August

Unbreak My Heart
Dar Tomlinson
ISBN-13: 978-1-58571-315-8
ISBN-10: 1-58571-315-5
$6.99

All I Ask
Barbara Keaton
ISBN-13: 978-1-58571-316-5
ISBN-10: 1-58571-316-3
$6.99

September

Icie
Pamela Leigh Starr
ISBN-13: 978-1-58571-275-5
ISBN-10: 1-58571-275-2
$6.99

At Last
Lisa Riley
ISBN-13: 978-1-58571-276-2
ISBN-10: 1-58571-276-0
$6.99

October

Everlastin' Love
Gay G. Gunn
ISBN-13: 978-1-58571-277-9
ISBN-10: 1-58571-277-9
$6.99

Three Wishes
Seressia Glass
ISBN-13: 978-1-58571-278-6
ISBN-10: 1-58571-278-7
$6.99

November

Yesterday Is Gone
Beverly Clark
ISBN-13: 978-1-58571-279-3
ISBN-10: 1-58571-279-5
$6.99

Again My Love
Kayla Perrin
ISBN-13: 978-1-58571-280-9
ISBN-10: 1-58571-280-9
$6.99

December

Office Policy
A.C. Arthur
ISBN-13: 978-1-58571-281-6
ISBN-10: 1-58571-281-7
$6.99

Rendezvous With Fate
Jeanne Sumerix
ISBN-13: 978-1-58571-283-3
ISBN-10: 1-58571-283-3
$6.99

2008 New Mass Market Titles

January

Where I Want To Be
Maryam Diaab
ISBN-13: 978-1-58571-268-7
ISBN-10: 1-58571-268-X
$6.99

Never Say Never
Michele Cameron
ISBN-13: 978-1-58571-269-4
ISBN-10: 1-58571-269-8
$6.99

February

Stolen Memories
Michele Sudler
ISBN-13: 978-1-58571-270-0
ISBN-10: 1-58571-270-1
$6.99

Dawn's Harbor
Kymberly Hunt
ISBN-13: 978-1-58571-271-7
ISBN-10: 1-58571-271-X
$6.99

March

Undying Love
Renee Alexis
ISBN-13: 978-1-58571-272-4
ISBN-10: 1-58571-272-8
$6.99

Blame It On Paradise
Crystal Hubbard
ISBN-13: 978-1-58571-273-1
ISBN-10: 1-58571-273-6
$6.99

April

When A Man Loves A Woman
La Connie Taylor-Jones
ISBN-13: 978-1-58571-274-8
ISBN-10: 1-58571-274-4
$6.99

Choices
Tammy Williams
ISBN-13: 978-1-58571-300-4
ISBN-10: 1-58571-300-7
$6.99

May

Dream Runner
Gail McFarland
ISBN-13: 978-1-58571-317-2
ISBN-10: 1-58571-317-1
$6.99

Southern Fried Standards
S.R. Maddox
ISBN-13: 978-1-58571-318-9
ISBN-10: 1-58571-318-X
$6.99

June

Looking for Lily
Africa Fine
ISBN-13: 978-1-58571-319-6
ISBN-10: 1-58571-319-8
$6.99

Bliss, Inc.
Chamein Canton
ISBN-13: 978-1-58571-325-7
ISBN-10: 1-58571-325-2
$6.99

2008 New Mass Market Titles (continued)

July

Love's Secrets
Yolanda McVey
ISBN-13: 978-1-58571-321-9
ISBN-10: 1-58571-321-X
$6.99

Things Forbidden
Maryam Diaab
ISBN-13: 978-1-58571-327-1
ISBN-10: 1-58571-327-9
$6.99

August

Storm
Pamela Leigh Starr
ISBN-13: 978-1-58571-323-3
ISBN-10: 1-58571-323-6
$6.99

Passion's Furies
AlTonya Washington
ISBN-13: 978-1-58571-324-0
ISBN-10: 1-58571-324-4
$6.99

September

Three Doors Down
Michele Sudler
ISBN-13: 978-1-58571-332-5
ISBN-10: 1-58571-332-5
$6.99

Mr Fix-It
Crystal Hubbard
ISBN-13: 978-1-58571-326-4
ISBN-10: 1-58571-326-0
$6.99

October

Moments of Clarity
Michele Cameron
ISBN-13: 978-1-58571-330-1
ISBN-10: 1-58571-330-9
$6.99

Lady Preacher
K.T. Richey
ISBN-13: 978-1-58571-333-2
ISBN-10: 1-58571-333-3
$6.99

November

This Life Isn't Perfect Holla
Sandra Foy
ISBN: 978-1-58571-331-8
ISBN-10: 1-58571-331-7
$6.99

Promises Made
Bernice Layton
ISBN-13: 978-1-58571-334-9
ISBN-10: 1-58571-334-1
$6.99

December

A Voice Behind Thunder
Carrie Elizabeth Greene
ISBN-13: 978-1-58571-329-5
ISBN-10: 1-58571-329-5
$6.99

The More Things Change
Chamein Canton
ISBN-13: 978-1-58571-328-8
ISBN-10: 1-58571-328-7
$6.99

Other Genesis Press, Inc. Titles

A Dangerous Deception	J.M. Jeffries	$8.95
A Dangerous Love	J.M. Jeffries	$8.95
A Dangerous Obsession	J.M. Jeffries	$8.95
A Drummer's Beat to Mend	Kei Swanson	$9.95
A Happy Life	Charlotte Harris	$9.95
A Heart's Awakening	Veronica Parker	$9.95
A Lark on the Wing	Phyliss Hamilton	$9.95
A Love of Her Own	Cheris F. Hodges	$9.95
A Love to Cherish	Beverly Clark	$8.95
A Risk of Rain	Dar Tomlinson	$8.95
A Taste of Temptation	Reneé Alexis	$9.95
A Twist of Fate	Beverly Clark	$8.95
A Will to Love	Angie Daniels	$9.95
Acquisitions	Kimberley White	$8.95
Across	Carol Payne	$12.95
After the Vows (Summer Anthology)	Leslie Esdaile T.T. Henderson Jacqueline Thomas	$10.95
Again My Love	Kayla Perrin	$10.95
Against the Wind	Gwynne Forster	$8.95
All I Ask	Barbara Keaton	$8.95
Always You	Crystal Hubbard	$6.99
Ambrosia	T.T. Henderson	$8.95
An Unfinished Love Affair	Barbara Keaton	$8.95
And Then Came You	Dorothy Elizabeth Love	$8.95
Angel's Paradise	Janice Angelique	$9.95
At Last	Lisa G. Riley	$8.95
Best of Friends	Natalie Dunbar	$8.95
Beyond the Rapture	Beverly Clark	$9.95
Blaze	Barbara Keaton	$9.95
Blood Lust	J. M. Jeffries	$9.95
Blood Seduction	J.M. Jeffries	$9.95

Other Genesis Press, Inc. Titles (continued)

Bodyguard	Andrea Jackson	$9.95
Boss of Me	Diana Nyad	$8.95
Bound by Love	Beverly Clark	$8.95
Breeze	Robin Hampton Allen	$10.95
Broken	Dar Tomlinson	$24.95
By Design	Barbara Keaton	$8.95
Cajun Heat	Charlene Berry	$8.95
Careless Whispers	Rochelle Alers	$8.95
Cats & Other Tales	Marilyn Wagner	$8.95
Caught in a Trap	Andre Michelle	$8.95
Caught Up In the Rapture	Lisa G. Riley	$9.95
Cautious Heart	Cheris F Hodges	$8.95
Chances	Pamela Leigh Starr	$8.95
Cherish the Flame	Beverly Clark	$8.95
Class Reunion	Irma Jenkins/ John Brown	$12.95
Code Name: Diva	J.M. Jeffries	$9.95
Conquering Dr. Wexler's Heart	Kimberley White	$9.95
Corporate Seduction	A.C. Arthur	$9.95
Crossing Paths, Tempting Memories	Dorothy Elizabeth Love	$9.95
Crush	Crystal Hubbard	$9.95
Cypress Whisperings	Phyllis Hamilton	$8.95
Dark Embrace	Crystal Wilson Harris	$8.95
Dark Storm Rising	Chinelu Moore	$10.95
Daughter of the Wind	Joan Xian	$8.95
Deadly Sacrifice	Jack Kean	$22.95
Designer Passion	Dar Tomlinson Diana Richeaux	$8.95
Do Over	Celya Bowers	$9.95
Dreamtective	Liz Swados	$5.95

Other Genesis Press, Inc. Titles (continued)

Ebony Angel	Deatri King-Bey	$9.95
Ebony Butterfly II	Delilah Dawson	$14.95
Echoes of Yesterday	Beverly Clark	$9.95
Eden's Garden	Elizabeth Rose	$8.95
Eve's Prescription	Edwina Martin Arnold	$8.95
Everlastin' Love	Gay G. Gunn	$8.95
Everlasting Moments	Dorothy Elizabeth Love	$8.95
Everything and More	Sinclair Lebeau	$8.95
Everything but Love	Natalie Dunbar	$8.95
Falling	Natalie Dunbar	$9.95
Fate	Pamela Leigh Starr	$8.95
Finding Isabella	A.J. Garrotto	$8.95
Forbidden Quest	Dar Tomlinson	$10.95
Forever Love	Wanda Y. Thomas	$8.95
From the Ashes	Kathleen Suzanne Jeanne Sumerix	$8.95
Gentle Yearning	Rochelle Alers	$10.95
Glory of Love	Sinclair LeBeau	$10.95
Go Gentle into that Good Night	Malcom Boyd	$12.95
Goldengroove	Mary Beth Craft	$16.95
Groove, Bang, and Jive	Steve Cannon	$8.99
Hand in Glove	Andrea Jackson	$9.95
Hard to Love	Kimberley White	$9.95
Hart & Soul	Angie Daniels	$8.95
Heart of the Phoenix	A.C. Arthur	$9.95
Heartbeat	Stephanie Bedwell-Grime	$8.95
Hearts Remember	M. Loui Quezada	$8.95
Hidden Memories	Robin Allen	$10.95
Higher Ground	Leah Latimer	$19.95
Hitler, the War, and the Pope	Ronald Rychiak	$26.95
How to Write a Romance	Kathryn Falk	$18.95

Other Genesis Press, Inc. Titles (continued)

I Married a Reclining Chair	Lisa M. Fuhs	$8.95
I'll Be Your Shelter	Giselle Carmichael	$8.95
I'll Paint a Sun	A.J. Garrotto	$9.95
Icie	Pamela Leigh Starr	$8.95
Illusions	Pamela Leigh Starr	$8.95
Indigo After Dark Vol. I	Nia Dixon/Angelique	$10.95
Indigo After Dark Vol. II	Dolores Bundy/ Cole Riley	$10.95
Indigo After Dark Vol. III	Montana Blue/ Coco Morena	$10.95
Indigo After Dark Vol. IV	Cassandra Colt/	$14.95
Indigo After Dark Vol. V	Delilah Dawson	$14.95
Indiscretions	Donna Hill	$8.95
Intentional Mistakes	Michele Sudler	$9.95
Interlude	Donna Hill	$8.95
Intimate Intentions	Angie Daniels	$8.95
It's Not Over Yet	J.J. Michael	$9.95
Jolie's Surrender	Edwina Martin-Arnold	$8.95
Kiss or Keep	Debra Phillips	$8.95
Lace	Giselle Carmichael	$9.95
Last Train to Memphis	Elsa Cook	$12.95
Lasting Valor	Ken Olsen	$24.95
Let Us Prey	Hunter Lundy	$25.95
Lies Too Long	Pamela Ridley	$13.95
Life Is Never As It Seems	J.J. Michael	$12.95
Lighter Shade of Brown	Vicki Andrews	$8.95
Love Always	Mildred E. Riley	$10.95
Love Doesn't Come Easy	Charlyne Dickerson	$8.95
Love Unveiled	Gloria Greene	$10.95
Love's Deception	Charlene Berry	$10.95
Love's Destiny	M. Loui Quezada	$8.95
Mae's Promise	Melody Walcott	$8.95

Other Genesis Press, Inc. Titles (continued)

Magnolia Sunset	Giselle Carmichael	$8.95
Many Shades of Gray	Dyanne Davis	$6.99
Matters of Life and Death	Lesego Malepe, Ph.D.	$15.95
Meant to Be	Jeanne Sumerix	$8.95
Midnight Clear (Anthology)	Leslie Esdaile Gwynne Forster Carmen Green Monica Jackson	$10.95
Midnight Magic	Gwynne Forster	$8.95
Midnight Peril	Vicki Andrews	$10.95
Misconceptions	Pamela Leigh Starr	$9.95
Montgomery's Children	Richard Perry	$14.95
My Buffalo Soldier	Barbara B. K. Reeves	$8.95
Naked Soul	Gwynne Forster	$8.95
Next to Last Chance	Louisa Dixon	$24.95
No Apologies	Seressia Glass	$8.95
No Commitment Required	Seressia Glass	$8.95
No Regrets	Mildred E. Riley	$8.95
Not His Type	Chamein Canton	$6.99
Nowhere to Run	Gay G. Gunn	$10.95
O Bed! O Breakfast!	Rob Kuehnle	$14.95
Object of His Desire	A. C. Arthur	$8.95
Office Policy	A. C. Arthur	$9.95
Once in a Blue Moon	Dorianne Cole	$9.95
One Day at a Time	Bella McFarland	$8.95
One in A Million	Barbara Keaton	$6.99
One of These Days	Michele Sudler	$9.95
Outside Chance	Louisa Dixon	$24.95
Passion	T.T. Henderson	$10.95
Passion's Blood	Cherif Fortin	$22.95
Passion's Journey	Wanda Y. Thomas	$8.95
Past Promises	Jahmel West	$8.95

Other Genesis Press, Inc. Titles (continued)

Path of Fire	T.T. Henderson	$8.95
Path of Thorns	Annetta P. Lee	$9.95
Peace Be Still	Colette Haywood	$12.95
Picture Perfect	Reon Carter	$8.95
Playing for Keeps	Stephanie Salinas	$8.95
Pride & Joi	Gay G. Gunn	$8.95
Promises to Keep	Alicia Wiggins	$8.95
Quiet Storm	Donna Hill	$10.95
Reckless Surrender	Rochelle Alers	$6.95
Red Polka Dot in a World of Plaid	Varian Johnson	$12.95
Reluctant Captive	Joyce Jackson	$8.95
Rendezvous with Fate	Jeanne Sumerix	$8.95
Revelations	Cheris F. Hodges	$8.95
Rivers of the Soul	Leslie Esdaile	$8.95
Rocky Mountain Romance	Kathleen Suzanne	$8.95
Rooms of the Heart	Donna Hill	$8.95
Rough on Rats and Tough on Cats	Chris Parker	$12.95
Secret Library Vol. 1	Nina Sheridan	$18.95
Secret Library Vol. 2	Cassandra Colt	$8.95
Secret Thunder	Annetta P. Lee	$9.95
Shades of Brown	Denise Becker	$8.95
Shades of Desire	Monica White	$8.95
Shadows in the Moonlight	Jeanne Sumerix	$8.95
Sin	Crystal Rhodes	$8.95
Small Whispers	Annetta P. Lee	$6.99
So Amazing	Sinclair LeBeau	$8.95
Somebody's Someone	Sinclair LeBeau	$8.95
Someone to Love	Alicia Wiggins	$8.95
Song in the Park	Martin Brant	$15.95
Soul Eyes	Wayne L. Wilson	$12.95

Other Genesis Press, Inc. Titles (continued)

Soul to Soul	Donna Hill	$8.95
Southern Comfort	J.M. Jeffries	$8.95
Still the Storm	Sharon Robinson	$8.95
Still Waters Run Deep	Leslie Esdaile	$8.95
Stolen Kisses	Dominiqua Douglas	$9.95
Stories to Excite You	Anna Forrest/Divine	$14.95
Subtle Secrets	Wanda Y. Thomas	$8.95
Suddenly You	Crystal Hubbard	$9.95
Sweet Repercussions	Kimberley White	$9.95
Sweet Sensations	Gwendolyn Bolton	$9.95
Sweet Tomorrows	Kimberly White	$8.95
Taken by You	Dorothy Elizabeth Love	$9.95
Tattooed Tears	T. T. Henderson	$8.95
The Color Line	Lizzette Grayson Carter	$9.95
The Color of Trouble	Dyanne Davis	$8.95
The Disappearance of Allison Jones	Kayla Perrin	$5.95
The Fires Within	Beverly Clark	$9.95
The Foursome	Celya Bowers	$6.99
The Honey Dipper's Legacy	Pannell-Allen	$14.95
The Joker's Love Tune	Sidney Rickman	$15.95
The Little Pretender	Barbara Cartland	$10.95
The Love We Had	Natalie Dunbar	$8.95
The Man Who Could Fly	Bob & Milana Beamon	$18.95
The Missing Link	Charlyne Dickerson	$8.95
The Mission	Pamela Leigh Starr	$6.99
The Perfect Frame	Beverly Clark	$9.95
The Price of Love	Sinclair LeBeau	$8.95
The Smoking Life	Ilene Barth	$29.95
The Words of the Pitcher	Kei Swanson	$8.95
Three Wishes	Seressia Glass	$8.95
Ties That Bind	Kathleen Suzanne	$8.95

Other Genesis Press, Inc. Titles (continued)

Tiger Woods	Libby Hughes	$5.95
Time is of the Essence	Angie Daniels	$9.95
Timeless Devotion	Bella McFarland	$9.95
Tomorrow's Promise	Leslie Esdaile	$8.95
Truly Inseparable	Wanda Y. Thomas	$8.95
Two Sides to Every Story	Dyanne Davis	$9.95
Unbreak My Heart	Dar Tomlinson	$8.95
Uncommon Prayer	Kenneth Swanson	$9.95
Unconditional Love	Alicia Wiggins	$8.95
Unconditional	A.C. Arthur	$9.95
Until Death Do Us Part	Susan Paul	$8.95
Vows of Passion	Bella McFarland	$9.95
Wedding Gown	Dyanne Davis	$8.95
What's Under Benjamin's Bed	Sandra Schaffer	$8.95
When Dreams Float	Dorothy Elizabeth Love	$8.95
When I'm With You	LaConnie Taylor-Jones	$6.99
Whispers in the Night	Dorothy Elizabeth Love	$8.95
Whispers in the Sand	LaFlorya Gauthier	$10.95
Who's That Lady?	Andrea Jackson	$9.95
Wild Ravens	Altonya Washington	$9.95
Yesterday Is Gone	Beverly Clark	$10.95
Yesterday's Dreams, Tomorrow's Promises	Reon Laudat	$8.95
Your Precious Love	Sinclair LeBeau	$8.95

Order Form

Mail to: Genesis Press, Inc.
P.O. Box 101
Columbus, MS 39703

Name ____________________
Address ____________________
City/State ____________________ Zip ____________________
Telephone ____________________

Ship to (if different from above)
Name ____________________
Address ____________________
City/State ____________________ Zip ____________________
Telephone ____________________

Credit Card Information
Credit Card # ____________________ ☐Visa ☐Mastercard
Expiration Date (mm/yy) ____________________ ☐AmEx ☐Discover

Qty.	Author	Title	Price	Total

Use this order form, or call 1-888-INDIGO-1

Total for books ____________________
Shipping and handling:
$5 first two books,
$1 each additional book ____________________
Total S & H ____________________
Total amount enclosed ____________________

Mississippi residents add 7% sales tax

Visit www.genesis-press.com for latest releases and excerpts.